SHADOWS OF THE PAST!!!

NIKITA BISHT

FOR MY LOVING LATE GRANDMA

You Made Me Fall In Love With Storytelling
Then And Now Forever!

Contents

Prologue

"Here, put that down."

"What are you talking about?" as I sipped the last of my tea.

"Your guilt, your past that you still carry in your head," he was trying to break me down.

"What are you feeling guilty about? Just don't stress yourself out. Don't be so overly concerned about me," as I kept the cup on the table next to me, giving him a look of disparage.

The man stopped and couldn't speak further. He was a friend to me, and that's what made him worry all the time. But sometimes, he was a jealous moron in disguise. He walked off my office room, and I didn't stop him. It wasn't arrogance or ego, but sometimes it is better not to disclose everything you have in your heart and mind to those who are just ready to spill your beans out in mass.

I stared at the letter lying on my desk with no name on it. We often have stories and identities that we seldom keep with ourselves, not letting the world know who we were and who we are.

Don't judge my past or present; you have your own life to handle first.

"You know what happened there. A few years back, you remember that, right," as the man returned to address me again while I was sitting in complete solitude.

"You know it, right? It was you who did it if I am not wrong," emphasised the agitated young man.

"Why don't you mind your own business? Look, fellow, if you are here to argue or fight out things, I am sorry, it's definitely not a day for it today," as I walked up to the bookshelf that cornered my bestsellers of all time.

I am a young, brave man, quite well-built, as people say, and I seldom had any interest in knocking off people, but I might get into one these days since haters pop up from anywhere you know.

He wasn't definitely my hater, but recently, things had changed. He was living on old roots, and that had made his notion a rebelling revolt for me.

"YOU ARE HIDING SOMETHING THERE! You are hiding behind your creations. You are so selfish and mean to let the people's world burn down. You live on those pieces of sympathy, but deep down, you know what happened that day," cried the man while yelling at the top of his voice.

I kept quiet and didn't lose my calm. It was not easy for me to recall something I never would have loved to discuss. But patience has come to me with years and losses that I wear like a badge in my life. I knew he was mad at me. I knew he was in pain. The agony of his was spilling out harsh words more than truth.

"Why are you not speaking up now? You said you had reasons, but why can't you be vocal about any of it, just a single of it," he chose to argue rather than to sit and hear.

I chose not to react to any of his emotions and actions, for I knew he was here to oppose and not to get the real answers anymore. He was fuming with anger, and all I could offer him at the moment was complete silence. I was going through the latest creation of mine to avoid the disturbance created in the air. He could definitely sense that I was already out of it, so at last, he gave up and went on his way.

I pulled out my favourite work from the collection and sat down again on my resting chair to go down memory lane. I was just turning the pages of the art prescription when I heard the sirens of a police van in the neighbourhood. I closed the book and left it on the desk to see what was going on outside. It was a rainy day, and all I could see was my foggy windowpane, which I tend to clear in order to have a glance at the outer world. The sirens and the light of it were flashing on the window. I remember those visions that came up fresh in my mind again. I could remember the white shroud hiding in my world. The hurried footsteps, the wailing, and the rain were breaking through the period of silent contemplation. The world was at a halt, and all I could do was stare through my foggy window.

(Knock…Knock)

"Sir, there is someone to see you," interrupted by a voice from behind, just standing at the door. I asked the office boy to let them in while still facing the window. I knew it was the time to shred off all I had in there, and yes, the world was waiting for things to change and to be kept aside.

A man in uniform appeared in the room and took the seat I had offered him.

"Long time, Mr. David; I hope you are doing well," smirked the policeman.

"Yes, Sir, very well. How can I help you, Sir?" I asked him while we exchanged a moment of silence for a few seconds. I knew him, and he knew me too, very well and from long ago.

We kept our stare game aside to get on to the business.

"Well, that's so kind of you. We had an interrogation going on regarding a case in your neighbourhood. I hope you will get along well," he said in a low, firm tone.

"Go ahead, Sir. I hope I will be useful to you," I smiled.

"There is a murder case in your neighbourhood. We just need you to stay in the town like all the neighbours. It's necessary if you stick with us for the interrogation," said the duty man while getting up from the seat.

With each step of his leaving my premises, I could recall the life living its body slowly and slowly, and then it never came back. Life is so precious to revive again… It was certain something was waiting for me there!

<h1>CHAPTER 1</h1>

"My Dear Tim" – Let's Begin!

"Do you believe in supernatural presence or powers? Do you? I don't… but I love creating stories about them. Well, let me introduce myself… I am David, a writer by profession, a preacher by conscience and a truly mad lover of fictional characters that I gave birth to every day."

"Sir, tea…" baffled by the voice of my housekeeper-Tim.

"Hmm? Oh… Okay, just keep it there." And I continued writing my stuff. Tim has been with me for the past two years. He is a living- dead lean character, ghosting around in my life. He is a very funny and amusing sweetheart, helping me out to survive in this old vintage wrecked house, too wrecked to be counted in the heritage list. Tim and I shifted to this place a month ago in search of inspiration and peace for deadly spooky creations. He believes I create wonders, and he is absolutely right since I have been writing thousands of stories that will make you feel chills running downright deep into your spine.

It feels as if Tim and I are companions for living ages, but he is a bit timid and superstitious about a lot of things. He believes my creations can be true in some other holy world of his that exists in his innocent little head. And then he warns me everytime I mimic his wobbly voice after hearing my masterpieces. Adding on to his fright, our new house, though not so new in real life, helps him to support his beliefs with all those cranky noises created by the old wooden floor. Somebody told me - hills hide stories... unnatural... so I came here with my buddy, or you can call him my little brother, to make it my new book's chapter. It's a beautiful place under a tranquil blue sky with pine woods surrounding our lush green lawn. I wish I was a dog lover too, to play all day in my tiny new garden.

Everything seems so mesmerising here except for our crooked house and the suspicious, weird neighbours who live next door across a stretch from our lawn. We never had a chance to visit their place for greetings, but it's their washed clothes clinging on the ropes almost every day that makes us believe we still have humans around.

"I was thinking, Tim, why don't I write a story for you this time after all you have been pondering about all my creepy narratives? Think of it...you will get a chance to eliminate the dark entities just like a superhero," me in a delightful tone, teasing my little brother. Tim in a very shy yet firm voice, "I believe Sir then you will have to keep the monsters a bit weak to get defeated by me." "Hahah," we both laughed. Tim never complains of the things the world did to him, and at times, I envy his patience and perseverance. His parents had long left him with his aunt who took no time in selling off the young flesh to brokers of this harsh cruel world. He has since then worked despite being of very tender young age and sending all the money he gets to his greedy spooky aunt. He is fifteen, and he has just studied till third standard and now no longer wishes to continue. He feels his aunt was miserable enough to send him to work despite knowing the fact that she had two elder sons who could do the earnings for their family. Poor Tim, he believes everyone, probably anyone and anything....

We get to hear birds chirping in our new world everyday with no sign of humans roaming about. I keep myself engrossed in my world and feel sorry for my buddy who has to accompany this lunatic to a place like this. God knows what made this little guy cling to me, for two long years. He hates my stories and yet loves them at the same time. Our new oldie house is said to have been abandoned by a very prominent Army General, years ago and we can sense that through the walls and the structures within the house that hold the very essence of his. This house is a beautiful architectural piece with intriguing wooden design with a Victorian and traditional touch of local elements as well. All I hate about it is the cranky wooden floors though they are a great help in case of someone sneaking in secretly. That's why we don't own a dog yet, we have our wooden floor guarding us so well. Jokes apart, we haven't seen many humans in our world since we last shifted here. It's just Tim and me, and I feel pity for him all the time.

"Sir, what story are we reading today… is it too scary?" asked a bit tensed Tim.

"No worries, buddy, we can skip our session for today if you want," I told him.

"No… I am ready to hear, I am just curious," said Tim in a very anxious voice.

It's our evening story time and we both sit in the bedroom upstairs every day with my buddy sitting next to me on the ground while I relax on the armchair instead. He never sits on a chair. He has a strange notion of admiring me as his giver of life and he says he takes me as his God, although I have scolded him a lot at times for this. For him I am always a hero unafraid of evil or anything and a person who he can rely on whenever he is scared.

"Well if you insist …let me help you with the latest creation of mine…. 'PHANTOM GUILT: SHADOWS OF THE PAST!!!,"

As I started with my narration, Tim leapt on to the side arm of my chair with his curious eyes staring at me.

"Some worlds away from the world of science and technology, homes the most unnatural and unreal truths that mankind has no explanation about. A world full of energies that are beyond imagination and yet to be discovered by the human world. A world is hidden in the dark yet wild natural habitat, where there once lived an old lady all alone. All she had was her miseries lingering on her and her alcoholic habit that made her still choose her life. She was dead inside, but something kept her living for ages. People called her a maniac … a witch … the creator of black magic…"

"Sir…" interrupted by my little fellow's innocent query, "Are the hills really a home for black magic?"

"I mean…Have you ever experienced black magic?" asked Tim.

"Aah… well, you know, Tim, these things are just to create an interest in stories… they are not as real as you see," I replied with a sigh.

"You should not take them to heart or even in your head dear. There happens to be no witch or black magic anywhere as of now in today's world. But if you will hear them as just stories, I bet it might thrill you brother."

It was almost dinner time now and we had to end our session for today since this holy kid was a bit engrossed in the topic of the day itself, so I had to put it at halt. You know how kids are … they often lead a life created in their head and I never want my Tim to believe in things that really have no existence other than in a fictional world.

We prepare food together and that's the best time I believe I get to spend with him after my narration period. Tim helps me in everything, but I want him to learn things that will help him sustain his life more than mine. My life now homes my creations- my books and also the best companion-Tim that I could ever ask for. His tender fingers at work make me think about the worldly wrong doings to the innocent little souls that suffer due to their fate or evil people around. It reminds me of the poor suffering since they are born.

(THUD… sounds of the window banging).

"Oh, Tim could you please go upstairs and close the window, it seems it is going to rain heavily tonight," as I looked out of my kitchen window, I could see the clothes next door still hanging to the rope swaying with the wind. I wonder if they knew it's going to rain after all. The tiny water droplets started drooling down the kitchen window reminding me of the day when I first met Tim. It was a rainy day indeed in the city with traffic on the road and me looking out of my car's window. It was then when I saw those tiny hands trying to knock at the front door glass and asking me to buy his pens. His clothes were drenched in water but all I could see was his pale face wearing a smile filled with hope. And now is this day I could at least bless him with a shelter and a home in his words. I smiled.

"Sir…should we start up with our dinner. It's tasty when it's hot."

I turned my eyes away from the window and saw my little boy standing behind me with a smile, but this time filled with joy and care.

"Sure," I smiled back.

As I looked back again at the neighbours, I saw a half-opened door and it seemed they were keeping an eye on us but the door was shut as soon as I looked at them whoever it was. STRANGE… nobody bothered to take the clothes inside though. This made me a bit curious. Although that night we had a pleasant time having dinner with the stormy weather outside. It was thundering and we had to keep up with an emergency light since the lights went off.

Knock Knock – I am Here!

The Sun was as usual out this morning and the Earth looked rejoiced by the tiny wake up droplets that were still there on the grass. The dew ornamented the leaves with its pearly presence. It seemed like a whole new day with a whole new place, so refreshing and soothing for the eyes. The unmistakable petrichor is one of my weaknesses after a rainy day working its spell so well to start a wonderful morning.

"Good morning, Sir," an unfamiliar voice from behind. As I turned back to see the speaker in person, I almost tripped over the pebble lying unnoticed in my tiny lawn.

"Oh Jesus … careful Sir," the stranger grabbed my arm to balance me.

"Thank Goodness, bless you. I am afraid, do I know you young fellow?" as I looked back at the saviour of the moment.

"I believe… no Sir. We are meeting for the first time. I delivered newspapers with my father in this area, and he was quite unwell to continue his job. So here I am to support him. Would you like to have our services for the same, Sir? We would be glad to serve you."

"Yeah, that would be great to keep up with today's world. Well you can join us for our morning tea to start with," as I pointed towards Tim, approaching us with the tea kettle.

"That's my little brother Tim, a cheerful young lad to survive with. Here Tim, you can place it down," directed by my voice, he kept the tea on the table.

"What did you say your name young fella," I asked the newspaper guy.

"Ben Sir, folks call me Benny. That's very kind of you for inviting me for tea. I need to rush to other houses to complete my work Sir. It was nice meeting you," smiled our new friend in this new world of ours.

The boy left to go to the other houses. I could see him visiting our strange neighbours too. As I sipped my tea and stared at the next door, I felt a bit weird since the newspaper boy was invited inside the strange house though I couldn't catch sight of the host.

"Don't you think we should have a cup of tea with our neighbours too someday, Tim," still staring at the next door while sipping my tea.

"Well Sir, we can surely do that any day after all we don't see much of life around here," giggled my buddy.

Our neighbours seemed to be low-key, unaffected by the world around us. They never happen to show themselves up in the open but their invite for Ben has put a full stop to my suspicious assumptions. Maybe they were nothing as we assumed or maybe more than that, you never know. As we say, "Never judge a book by its cover." Maybe someday we might get along to have some chit chats. They happen to spend much of their time indoors that usually confuses us of how many of them are actually residing in there. But they seem to have a great habit of cleaning laundry every third day. That helps me in guessing their number which I believe is around three to four family members' maybe.

"Sir, breakfast is ready. Should I bring it here for you?"

"No dear, I will come inside. We have a lot of work to do today," taking the last sip of my morning energy drink. Like any other tea lover, my mornings can never go without a cup of my ambrosia or amrita to be precise. These woods around our oldie home act the best scenario to enjoy my beginning of each day here. Tim loves woods too since he had never been to hills before this. This place adds to the best time of our life.

We had our morning meal and were all set to go with our daily routine. Suddenly the doorbell rang. Tim went to open the door but to our surprise there was no one present outside the door. We assumed it was a prank by someone around or some passer-by, so we continued with our work. I had to complete my on-going fictional piece now since that's what feeds me as a writer in general, so I went upstairs to continue my writing business. Tim was working downstairs with some everyday chores. I had my writing table beside the window looking into our lawn directing towards the next door too. The outside view helped me in refreshing my mind at times whenever I felt exhausted and drowsy most of the time. I was writing down my "PHANTOM GUILT!!" plot step by step and I wanted to make it a success someday. As I continued to write, I heard the doorbell rang once again and then I heard hurried footsteps going towards the door to open. All I could hear was the door open and with some pause in between the door closed again.

"Who's there Tim?"

"There is no one outside, Sir. I think someone is knowingly messing up with us," answered Tim from downstairs in a loud worried voice.

"Never mind there must be kids around, you can come up and relax in your room buddy. Don't work so much or else I will have to come down and help you anyway."

I had never been to such a calming place before and it was really helping me in my story. It seemed as if nature had a lot to say about its mysteries. I wonder if the army personnel would have enjoyed his best time here. You can never ignore the beauty and serenity the hills and mountains carry with them. The deep forests become deeper as you start gazing at them and they often helped me in diving in my imagination ocean. But as you know my genre is all about thrilling people and scaring them out of their skins, I have to often turn beauty into darkness-unrevealed and untouched. People often talk about the black magic rituals carried out in mountain regions which though in general I would have refuted but since that's how my work works, it could be a great expedition to take up. So now you know, that's how my new project was taking its shape.

I was busy writing my holy volume and Tim was in his room taking some power nap. It was a pleasant afternoon by now, so I kept my notes aside and went to the kitchen downstairs to prepare our lunch. We had decided to have a kitchen garden too, so we had planted a few veggies around though they still had time to fully take their form. Maybe in a couple of days or weeks we might get to have our meal prepared with them. But for the time being, we had to shop our groceries from a market nearby- not so near for the people from the plains to be precise. You have to climb all the way up the hill to get to the closest shop and my legs don't really help me in that at all though people say I am very young to stick to this notion of mine. I think I need my kitchen garden to bloom real soon.

(DOORBELL RINGS)

"Ugh…who's that now? If one more pranks again, I am going to make sure he gets a hard lesson this time."

I went to check on the uninvited visitor. As soon as I opened the door, it was Ben, the newspaper guy.

"Oh hey, I thought someone was fooling around. I am glad it's you. Welcome dear," sighed in relief.

"Thank you, Sir, I hope I didn't disturb you. I was just passing by, so I thought of greeting you."

"No, not at all. Come inside please."

"Some other day Sir will be heading home now. There was a letter of yours Sir. Here, (A white envelope addressed to our bungalow no. 2468) it got to the other house mistakenly, so they gave it to me to pass on to you. You must be waiting for it."

"Thank you dear, sorry for bothering you for this. That's really so careless behaviour of the post guy. I should thank our neighbours too for keeping it safe."

The boy smiled and went off his way home. I kind of feel now our neighbours are not so tough to get along with. Anyways, I needed to finish off with my lunch duty since Tim would have been hungry by this time. It was almost four o'clock now, so I woke him up for the meal. The lunch was ready for two of us to pounce upon like two hungry tigers. Meanwhile, the envelope was lying on the shelf of the kitchen waiting for me to open and go through. We were done with our heavy late afternoon meal and were set to clean off the kitchen and the dishes.

It was time for me to have a look at the letter we had received as it had been quite a long time since we last heard from somebody. It could be a letter from my publisher I suppose because he was a constant guy who never lost my touch even if I wanted to. As I opened the envelope, something pricked my finger, and the blood stained the letter.

"Oh... how stupid to place a head pin to hold a single page letter. Let me see what it says now."

(The LETTER says)

DEAR FRIEND,

I AM GLAD YOU CAME. LET ME WELCOME YOU TO OUR WORLD. I KNOW YOU DON'T KNOW ME BUT LIFE IS TOO SHORT TO HAVE REAL INTRODUCTIONS MY FRIEND.I COULD HAVE WISHED FOR A BETTER FUTURE FOR YOU BUT YOU ARE ALREADY BEST AT YOUR PRESENT. MY WRITER FRIEND, STOP GUESSING NAMES WHO IS WRITING TO YOU. THAT'S NOT SO IMPORTANT TO KNOW RIGHT NOW. BUT I AM HERE TO HELP YOU LIVE BETTER AND LONGER THAN YOUR STORIES THAT YOU SELL OFF SO WELL. THERE IS A SECRET I KEEP... A SECRET THAT I WANT YOU TO KNOW SINCE YOU ARE ALREADY HERE. THOSE WOODS... THOSE WOODS ARE SHADY LIKE YOUR STORY... SO BE AWARE!!

THERE IS SOMEONE OUT THERE.SOMEONE SO UNREAL YET VERY POWERFUL. SOMEONE LOVES TO HUNT. SOMEONE LOVES TO TEAR MINDS APART. THE WOODS ARE DEADLY, DARK AND DEEP. DON'T PEEP INSIDE. REMEMBER, DON'T LOOK BACK. JUST SAVE YOURSELF!!! I SAID... JUST SAVE YOURSELF!!!!!

YOUR WELL WISHER

(THE SECRET KEEPER)

A strange chill went down the spine as I read the last lines. It seemed like a horrific joke, or something played on me. What a weird letter I could have expected as of now. Who was messing up for no reason?

"What has happened Sir?"

"Nothing, just a friend of mine writing to me after so long," as I looked back at Tim's curious face, not wanting him to know about it.

"Oh, that's so sweet you got to hear from him," smiled Tim while setting up the washed utensils.

I too smiled back and then went into the chain of deep thoughts while holding the letter in my hand.

Was it really a threat to my life? Was it real? I tried to read the letter thrice to make sure if I had read it correctly in the first place. I couldn't move for a moment. A weird feeling of numbness could be sensed within me. My feet froze to the ground and a sudden chill ran deep down my spine for a second. Was it a prank? Or was someone really warning me of something unknown?

I was deep rooted in my thoughts and worries and then all I could see was Tim running towards me. And then I saw my finger had started spilling a heavy flow of blood suddenly from nowhere making it very painful for me.

"Oh Sir ... what happened to your hand?" Tim was left in a bewildered state trying to stop the blood flow.

"Just a prick Tim ... it will be fine don't worry," as I saw him cleaning up the wound.

Just a prick though still the bleeding was making it appear as if one must have had a severe cut. STRANGE! How could a head pin cause such a severe injury? Strange, But for me, the letter had all my concern for the moment. I tried to find some clue or name on the envelope or in the letter itself to make out the sender's identification but couldn't find any.

There was an eerie feeling in the air. The complete silence was getting disturbed by the slow breathing sounds. I could hear the wall clock ticking, TICK - TOCK … TICK - TOCKK… TIICCKK … TOCCKK…which was gradually increasing in volume.

"Is everything alright Sir? You look so worried," the fellow's concerned voice interrupted my thought chain.

"Hmm. Yeah, everything is okay. Let us just wind up our chores for now. I will be going upstairs. I am a bit tired, you too take some rest," as I walked up the stairs heading to my room.

I was in my room now. I kept the letter on my writing desk and sat down on my chair to just stick to my daily grind. Everything was so normal, yet a weird uneasy feeling was pervading my work space - my mind. Was it a procrastination, I fear? Maybe it was. I opened the window in front of my desk to let the fresh air in.

The sky was clear blue; I could see the birds flying into the infinity of the blue stretch. And below that blue belt were the green dark forests giving a firm stare back at me. They were so natural and so serene to be part of nature that for once I felt how somebody could just portray a negative picture of them. I tried clearing out my mind and started to think about my work for which I was sitting at my writing desk in the first place. But all I could gather in my brain were the random thoughts ruining my working spirit. So I stopped and then I saw the letter that I had kept aside. Wasn't it strange to have no sender's address on it? It was becoming more like a headache for me as I couldn't stop noticing it lying on my desk. So I dumped it in one of my drawers for the time being. While I sat there in complete silence to rest my mind a bit, the woods were catching my sight now due to that unholy letter I received. So I closed the window and put on the curtains to bar the view in front and sat down quietly again.

(THUD… a loud noise of something hit on the windowpane)

"WHAT WAS THAT!!!" as I was taken aback by the sound.

I opened the curtain to see what had hit the glass but couldn't see anything. I opened the window and looked down to see what it was. There was something lying on the ground, but I could barely make out what exactly it was because of the distance. I hurried downstairs and went outside to check. While Tim too followed me as he also heard the sound that was quite loud and clear despite being in the other room. As we walked to the spot, Tim was feeling bad about what had happened.

"Oh God, poor little thing, how did it not see the window?" he felt sorry for the little creature.

I looked down at the dead sparrow that had hit the windowpane and was lying there still on the ground. It seemed so weird to even think of the reason for why the sparrow would have not noticed the house in the first place. Also it was appearing as if somebody threw it with greater force at the glass which would have actually not happened in real life. Why would somebody do that to a poor little life? I picked up the sparrow to bury it at a distance from our house in the corner of our lawn as we couldn't just leave it there to become someone's food any sooner. So I started digging a small pit though a bit deeper with the help of a masonry spade that I had in my store. Tim was standing next to me with his face drooping in sadness. He is quite a sensitive boy to take up such incidents to his heart though life is not always a happy story for all, and I wanted him to learn to accept a few things that are beyond our control.

My spade just hit something hard as I tried digging deeper. Maybe it was a stone or a rock, so I tried removing the mud to pull out the obstacle. But to my surprise, the thing was something shiny as I almost cleared the mud over it. I tried pulling it out and it was a small chest more like a jewellery box of some kind. Though, the box didn't appear to be very old as it was still having its shine. Also it was kind of made up of silver and this made me curious since it seemed to be valuable to me.

"What is it Sir? Don't touch it. What is it doing in our lawn?" Tim a bit tensed at the moment while looking at the chest.

I ignored his words while opening it to see what it was. But all I found in it was a bunch of head pins filling it up.

"Head pins? Who even puts that in a jewellery box and that too hides it under the ground? That's weird," Tim gave an ugly reaction to what we found.

I was quiet since I felt a bit weird to see that they were kind of the same headpins that the letter had attached to it. They were all having coloured tops like the one I had in my room's drawer. I didn't want to jump into conclusions or any other thoughts to declare if the letter had a real motive of harming me but somehow things weren't making sense and were quite puzzling me at the moment. So I just took it out and laid the bird in there to rest in peace. I then headed back to my house while Tim stopped me from behind.

"Wait Sir, are we going to take it inside? It could be anything, and I think we should throw it off."

"Anything like what, I didn't get you? It's just a box filled with head pins. It won't cause any harm if taken inside the house," me trying to play it cool while seeing the worried expression on Tim's face.

All I wanted was to see if it was the same pins as the one, I was having on the letter. Just a confirmation I needed the most at that time, but I couldn't explain it to him.

"But Sir...," paused the little guy.

"But what, what are you afraid of Tim? Just speak up, be clear," I tried comforting him.

"What if Sir, there is something wrong with it? I mean you only told once that some people drop unusual things at other's places to perform some kind of black magic. Maybe it's not black magic but still is it okay to carry it inside since we don't know why it was there in the first place?" asked the concerned voice.

"Oh God, Tim there is nothing like black magic dear I already told you that day. Those are just stories made up by people like me who love to scare the people out of their skins. Don't worry it's just a harmless box and that too of headpins," me trying to ease the little boy from his fear of fictional things.

"Also, maybe some kids must have hidden it while playing around. So don't think so much my dear," me holding Tim's hand to take him inside.

I didn't want my brother to indulge into superstitious beliefs, so it was kind of important for me now to take that box indoors to prove my point. Although it was very weird to even have it there in our lawn and for a second my mind too was running thoughts of such superstitious practices, but I stopped them at once. I took it to my room and when Tim was busy somewhere; I took out the letter to match the pin attached to it.

DAMN! It was the same! Was it really one of those pins? Was the letter from someone nearby me? But who could have done it and dumped it there? My head had again become a home of a number of stupid thoughts and questions. I was confused and worried at the same time not knowing what to assume from things that I just saw. My finger had started giving me severe pain in between to remind me of the existence of the wound that was supposed to be minor but was not looking like what it has to be anyhow.

It was turning dark by now and Tim was already back in the kitchen to prepare the dinner for the two of us. So I went downstairs to help him out with the same while keeping my worries aside for the time being. Also it was all time to laugh out and enjoy our meal together like everyday ritual. That night I slept late since my mind was not ready to rest at first and then slowly it fell asleep.

CHAPTER

3

The Old Post Office

"Time can heal wounds, but scars are always left behind." And here my wound had no mood of healing with time. My finger had swollen a lot and turned blue, making it hard for me to work at all. It was quite absurd to have such an injury from a very tiny thing. But as you know one should not be judged by its size though. Tragedies happen uninvited with anyone you see. So was my case, surprising yet painful at the same time. I wonder what caused this injury to worsen so much. Anyways it wasn't my concern at the first place maybe that's how it worked. It was day five and I was having an instinct of getting it checked up once. Though I felt it might be okay with time but since my presumptions weren't falling in place so I looked for the nearest clinic I could locate. Also the Letter you see, the letter I received days back had to be inquired about too. The letter had almost ruined my normal life. Also the mysterious box was too on my concern list.

So I decided to look for my answers and solve the mystery created here for it was really messing up with my working spirit now and that's what I couldn't afford to have.

"Here Tim, I will be leaving in a while to get some medical help. Just have your lunch done. I will be back in the evening," while I saw Tim in the kitchen.

"Sure Sir but I must suggest that you have your lunch first. You haven't had anything since morning."

"That's so sweet of you, my boy. But I will be late and will be heading somewhere to finish off some business of mine. You don't worry."

So I left for the clinic while putting the letter in my pocket and taking the mysterious box along. I was in the town street now looking for the address that I had with me. It was my first time in the town street and therefore I was quite not sure about the addresses and whereabouts of any of it. Also I found that the street was quite crowded with people busy moving here and there. I could see the street vendors on the sides of the road leading to somewhere which was not the matter of interest for me right now. I was looking at my swollen finger while walking up the street when suddenly an old lady bumped into me, and we almost lost balance with her bag falling on the ground while her belongings came out of her bag.

"Hell, now! Be careful young man! You almost scattered my stuff," the old lady mumbling while kneeling down to pick up her belongings.

I felt sorry for the situation and tried helping her while keeping my box on the ground and gathering the stuff lying around. She was quite annoyed by the bumping thing, but I managed to keep her calm while handing over the bag to her. So she left and I was ready to go my way when I suddenly found that something was missing. I tried looking everywhere on the street around me, but I couldn't find the box. Where did it go? I lost the box I was supposed to discover. That was so lame of me. I was still searching for it when a young boy came up to me asking if he could help me. I looked at him but didn't speak a word and continued searching for the lost box. He then noticed my swollen blue finger while still standing next to me.

"You should see a doctor. Your finger doesn't really look fine," said the boy in a concerned tone.

"Yeah, can you just tell me where would I get this address," while showing off the piece of paper I had jotted down the location on.

"That way, just turn to the left from the post office and then walk down the lane you will get the medico four shops down," directed the boy.

"Thank you, I wanted to visit the post office anyway and by luck, they are in the same direction. Thank you again and have a nice day my buddy," I smiled at the helpful kid.

I knew I wasn't getting the box back now, but I really had other things to do as well, so I walked off from there heading towards my destination. As I reached the hospital which was quite far and totally opposite to what I had assumed, I found that it hardly had any staff in there, which was really a matter of concern. I sat down in the waiting area and then after a couple minutes' wait, I saw a lady coming in dressed in white coat with a stethoscope around her neck. I was happy to see her, but it seemed she wasn't feeling the same for me though. So I sat down again waiting for her to call me inside for an examination. The place was quite unused with a lot of cleaning required. Maybe nobody visits here so frequently and that might explain the shortage of human power here. And then came out a man from inside directing me to the doctor's room.

"Here, come sit. Are you new here?" asked the lady sitting on the doctor's chair.

"Yes, madam, I just shifted a few days back in here. Actually I hurt my finger and it's becoming worse now," I explained to her.

She took a close look at the finger and then gave a stern look back at me. I didn't get what it was for, but I kept quiet to go with the flow at the moment. She then wrote down a few tests and I was accompanied by a nurse who appeared from nowhere taking me for the tests. I waited in the hall for the results praying for everything to be normal. I was then again called inside the doctor's cabin.

"You were most likely to develop gangrene if you'd come later. How did you even get hurt?" asked the doctor.

"I just got a prick by a headpin, and it wasn't that severe but now you see it looks critical as you say," the worried me spoke up in a trembling voice.

It really wasn't supposed to get this worse by such a small object but thank goodness I was saved for now. I took the necessary treatment and then walked home but then suddenly I remembered about the letter I was supposed to enquire about. So I went halfway back to the post office to clear out some of my doubts. I knocked at the door of the post office when I saw an old man sitting at the desk that was probably the only desk out there. He seemed to be working alone in this remote area. Although his appearance was quite friendly, he suddenly changed his body language as he noticed me at the doorstep.

"How can I help you Sir?" asked the curious postmaster.

"Good Afternoon Sir, actually I was here to enquire about a letter," I greeted him with a smile while taking out the letter from my pocket and placing it on the table in front of him.

He looked at the envelope and then he turned his head up.

"Yeah, go ahead," while examining the letter envelope closely.

"I got this letter, but it has no sender's name as you can see. So can you just help me tell who could possibly send it to me?" I am curious to get the answer in my favour and trying to figure out the post master's next move through his changing face expressions.

"How can I even tell that Sir since we get our letters from distant and us purely keeps an account of such letters with such errors, but I believe we got none like this before? By the way, I didn't recognise you. And I surely don't remember handing over such a letter to anyone recently," said the postmaster in a confused tone.

"Yeah, you handed it over to my neighbours by mistake which I am already ignoring about. Your mishandling of your job has kind of landed me into overthinking. So just let me know and we are well off thereafter as you see I am in no mood of complaining," as I tried to control my fury under the expression of forced smile.

"What rubbish are you trying to portray that I am not doing my job well? Listen, I don't hand over such anonymous letters to people. Okay? That's my god Damn job and I know how to do it well. And also what neighbours are you talking about? Who are you?" the postmaster lost his control.

"Hey, calm down. Relax. All I just want is the sender's name. If you don't know, that's fairly cool. Don't lose your temper on me for no reason. Okay?" as I backed off while seeing his expressions getting even worse than before.

It seemed as if the postmaster would have soon attacked me out of rage to just point out his irresponsible behaviour which totally was the main concern. But I was in no mood to just have a clash off at a new place for no reason, so I picked the letter and then left the room fully heated by the argument that had started in there.

I now started walking back home since it was quite a stressful day for me till now. It was weird for him to behave like a hooligan since it was really a big thing to have no records of such anonymous letters. I mean you only think how such letters with no names can build up curiosity and suspense in people for no reason. And this letter was not a normal letter; it was kind of a threat or a warning for someone like me who actually knew no one in this new place. Why would somebody become an enemy of mine without even knowing me? This was a really scary and very mind-boggling scenario to even digest. Also I meant no harm to anyone in here so why would somebody try to write me such letters that truly make no sense? The letter literally was making the woods appear to be kind of murderers like in whooping horror or thriller novels, which can only exist in an imaginary world and has nothing in common with the real one. Well I had to reach home first since it was evening by now and I needed to have some rest.

I could see Tim watering the plants in the garden when I was almost there. My feet stopped to admire him from a distance. He was such a hardworking and disciplined child which I wasn't at all when I was his age. I was happy to see him growing up so well like a gentleman at his best. So I smiled and stepped forward. My foot seemed to have stepped on something kind of soft and smooth, and as I looked at the ground, I saw that it was a dead bird.

"Oh, God, no, it can't happen again. Where did it come from?" I stepped aside to see what caused it to die.

Tim heard me and came running to see what had happened. He stood at a distance while staring at the dead creature.

"It's not good, Sir. The bird! It's a bad omen," said the boy in a worried low tone.

I looked at his face, which was turning pale, and that was concerning me now.

"NO, no, it's just normal; some dog must have attacked it. There is nothing to worry so much about. No Omen thing. No bad thing. I will just throw it off in the bushes since anyone can dig up the lawn to get it out," I tried to calm his mind through my words of assurance.

"You better get back and prepare some tea for the two of us. It was kind of a very tiring day today for me," I told Tim.

He was still looking at the bird while heading to the door. I could see him running serious thoughts in his innocent mind that weren't supposed to be there at all. I looked back at the bird as Tim went inside. Its eyes seemed to stare at me, and I could see the depth in them, so dark and so captivating that for a few seconds I didn't realise that I was staring at a dead body for so long. It had to be thrown away, as well as the thought, the concern, and the dead.

I then went inside to sip up the tasty energising drink that was my only cure to uneasy life outside. All I wanted was to stop my mind from running so fast at the moment. So we enjoyed our cup of tea together, me and Tim. I was happy to see him beside me so relaxed and enjoying it and I wanted to capture the moment, at least for now. Although my suffering had just begun. I continued sipping my tea, while placing my other hand in the pocket holding the death warrant of my happiness.

Conflicting Mind

As minutes, hours and days passed by; my concern was taking its deepest roots into my mind. My days were restless with no mood of continuing my writing work. It felt as if I had a lot of burden kept on my shoulders. Things weren't falling in place at all. My anxiety had become the master of my mind, and I had no other option other than making the first move to find out the truth behind all my sufferings. I knew no one in the town yet and it was all working against me. I was having the urge of meeting my neighbours to inquire if they knew something related to the letter of misery I received. The postmaster had already become an enemy to my words of fury and concern. As he said that he had no information regarding the letter, which was quite strange for me to digest. Also my mornings weren't the same anymore.

I saw Tim keeping up with chores. Those hands at work had sometimes been my pill to remorse.

"I have some work outside. Have your breakfast. I will have later," I told Tim.

"But Sir you haven't been eating well these days. Are you keeping well Sir? Is there something bothering you? I am sorry for asking you so many questions. But something seems to be wrong with you Sir."

"No, no there's nothing that you need to worry about, just busy with my inspiration hunt you know. You can put your mind at rest my buddy," as I smiled at those worried eyes.

"Also don't let in any uninvited being behind my back my lad. Since we don't really know people around here, so be alert. We've been hearing so much nuisance and cases of concern these days. So be careful."

"Done Sir," smiled Tim.

So I left and was standing outside in my lawn from where I could see the next door clearly - built so old similar to ours. I smiled as soon as I caught the sight of clothes hanging onto the rope outside their house as a part of their daily ritual. And then I caught a sudden sight of the ravens above the house next door, with one of them landing on their entrance gate working just perfectly like the eerie scenes of any haunted film. You know, they being the psychopomps acting as a bad omen are believed to be bringing death or illness with them, which I usually otherwise don't approve of though.

As I continued staring at the raven, I felt a sudden hypnotic power taking over me, slowly freezing my gaze at its dark eyes. The raven was staring right back at me, appearing to be in rage for some reason. Its deep-set black eyes were filled with fury and having thick bills made it appear like a griever of darkness for sure. The stare game was still going on when I felt a creepy cold grab over my shoulder with my body still frozen-my eyes still fixed at the ones staring me back. I felt like turning around for a moment, but some strange malign powers were making it hard for me to move even an inch. My body felt an unpleasant invisible weight stoop on it. And then I heard something murmur so low, it seemed like a cold mysterious breeze whispering into my ears, so cold, so hollow … so spine chilling - "SAVE YOURSELF, …. THE WOODS ARE DARKKK…"

I felt the cold touch move down slowly and slowly all over my back making my nerves clench in pain.

All I could see was the bird's eyes that were just getting deeper and deeper with time. The silence was being intruded by the ravens flying over the place seeming to mimic some unholy noises.

And then suddenly a deep voice came from behind that shooed the raven away.

For a moment it felt like I was coming out of the deep nasty sleep, the paralytic hypnosis state left off my body and it felt so light again.

"Are you fine Sir," the voice called again.

The voice seemed to be very familiar to me. I turned back and saw the young fellow staring at me with a bundle of newspapers in his hands.

"Oh hello Ben, when did you get here? I am sorry I didn't notice you."

"That's perfectly fine Sir. I have been here for a while. Are you looking for something Sir?"

"Oh no, it was just that… oh I was just strolling around as for morning walks. Ah as they make a good start for a day you see," my voice was shaking a bit with my lips trembling in confusion and fear.

Ugly thoughts had started creeping into my mind. Was it Ben the whole time? Should I ask him if it was, he who must have taken hold of me? But why would he do that?

I took a pause as my head started aching with endless thoughts and questions running in my mind.

"Was it you all the time? I mean I really didn't notice you. Was that your touch?"

"I didn't get you Sir. What touch?"

"Ah… Nothing, anyways you can hand over the newspaper to me. Thank you."

Was he lying? What was it exactly? If it wasn't him then who could it be? He had left already but my mind was still confused, filled with queries unanswered. A creepy feeling of being watched by somebody was still lingering in the air. I felt someone was still looking at me from a distance. As I looked at the woods at the back of my house, I saw a faint figure of someone standing behind one of the pine trees. I could barely figure out who it was and then the figure turned around and walked off while disappearing into the woods.

A nasty feeling took over me. It seemed as if the woods would open up its dark arms and would drag me into it. I had never seen the woods that way before so lonely, scary, and dark possessing my mind with its be-wilderness. The weather seems so gloomy today covered in dark clouds making no way for the sunshine.

I turned back towards the neighbourhood and walked silently, perplexed with all that happened a few minutes back. Maybe it could be some kind of hallucination due to the loss of appetite these days. Maybe the anxiety was making me see stupid things or maybe it was really someone pranking around just to mess up with my work or something. Maybe I was thinking a lot more than what was needed.

I walked straight to the front door of the neighbour's house facing our lawn and pushed the bell button which seemed to have lived for centuries by its appearance. The door seemed very old too, calling for a complete renovation. I could see some flowerpots at the doorstep which needed to be looked after and replaced since I could barely find any living plants in them. The dried stems of the plant were the very signs of not being attended for days or maybe months. There on the tiny nameplate was inscribed - "Parkins."

I rang the bell again since nobody came to attend the door. The clothes hanging over the rope were all white. Maybe they were having some kind of obsession with purity you see. I was busy noticing things, but nobody showed up. Even though there was no lock from outside, there was definitely someone inside. The wait was making me more anxious with all the questions I had in my mind regarding the letter. It was quite a few minutes now and it was making me feel uneasy and restless. How weird it was for them to be so obnoxiously unwelcoming to guests or visitors.

It was irritating me now and I desperately wanted to know the truth behind the letter. So I went around the house to see if I could see somebody in person as one can be busy working and not able to notice the bell chime. Though the bell had quite a loud sound to be noticed or heard but still there could be any possibilities and I wanted to inquire today itself about who actually handed over that wretched letter to them mistakenly.

There was not even a single person around the house nor in their garden which was not even trimmed probably since ages. These people were real creeps though to have been living like this since whenever. Maybe that's the reason why we don't see many visitors here.

As I was walking around, I saw a window with curtains aside. I had a feeling of peeping inside although it was breaching privacy and might not be liked by them at all but all that anxiety and curiosity of mine made me act unethically for the moment.

So I peeped inside to see if anyone was present there. As soon as I had a glance, something unnatural struck my eyes which baffled me at the moment. To my surprise I saw the place inside was pitch dark, too dark to even see anything at all as if it was nighttime and all lights were off which frightened me and shocked me for a moment. All I could barely figure out was a staircase in front of the window that must have led to the upper storey. And then suddenly something made a noise, a creaky noise of a door opening beside the staircase. My eyes weren't helping me enough to see what was happening inside and then I heard some slow footsteps coming out of the room having faint light. All I could see in the room was some candles burning and a shadow of someone which was making it clear that someone was inside. The footsteps sound felt like receding towards the main door and then suddenly it stopped. I was struggling to see if I could know what exactly was going on inside, but I couldn't make out what it was and who it was in person. All I could see was the shadow in the room flicking with the flicker of the candlelight. No wonder where would have that guy gone since the main gate didn't seem to open yet. The shadow inside the room was kneeling down and seemed to bow head on the floor. The figure was quite faint, so I leapt on the window closer for gazing clearly inside.

An old pale wrinkled face with fierce blood red eyes pounced right on me from inside with her nails scratching the window pane making a loud screeching noise and yelled out loud on my face - "I TOLD YOU ALREADY!!!! NO ONE LIVES HERE!!!!" Her skin was as deadly as a corpse.

I freaked out of my body and fell right on back hitting my head on something hard on the ground. That yell was so loud, so scary that it almost deafened my ears. All I could see were the stars twinkling in the sky. How could it be night by now since it hadn't been so long for me to be here? Was it not the daytime when I had been here in the first place? How could this be so true yet not so true? My mind was still painting the picture of the freaky old face. Her nails seemed to appear like old thick wood that could have almost scrunched my throat out if the glass barrier wouldn't have been there at all. I felt a sharp pain on the back of my head, my eyes getting dizzy. Slowly and slowly, I started losing consciousness. All I could see was the blurry night sky with my eyes closing to darkness unknown.

Chapter
5

Hush!!! She Is Awake!!

I heard a faint whining voice of concern bringing me back to my senses. I could feel tiny hands rubbing my chest and then someone holding my freezing hands. I saw a blurry face of someone I knew, that's my Tim. He was here to save me. My boy was here for me. I could see him clearly; I smiled at those teary eyes.

"Oh you Tim, how can I even live without you?"

"Your head is bleeding Sir, how did this happen? Oh Goodness, how will I make it stop now!!" I could see his anxious eyes looking at his stained hands supporting my head.

"How on Earth did you get here?" asked my anxiety.

"I was waiting for you, Sir. It's been a long day. I waited for you but you didn't return. I am so in pain to see you like this. What were you doing here?"

"I just came to see our neighbours," while trying to get up. My head was still giving me a hard time as I struggled moving myself.

"Wait Sir, don't move so much, let me call someone for help from inside," Tim directed in a pained, concerned voice.

"Oh no, no, no please don't go inside. She won't like it."

"Who Sir, did you meet someone?"

"Yes… I mean no. (Hesitating a bit) We shouldn't bother them much, it's already late. I will be fine. I can walk back home."

Tim helped me stand up on my feet again with my one arm clinging on his shoulder and the other covering the wound on my head. My heart was pounding so fast at the moment thinking of all that happened the whole day. My legs were still shaky and were moving with difficulty.

As we crossed the main doorway of the house, Tim noticed something.

"Sir there's a lock there. They wouldn't have been of any help to us anyway."

The door was locked!!! Was it the whole time? My body was turning cold with fear slowly and slowly as we were almost out of their premises. How could it be possible to even forget what I saw in there? How did I even get injured in the first place if it was all a dream or a nightmare to be precise?

But why did she say nobody lives there when there was somebody else too beside her. Who were they?

What were they doing in there? Or were they really in there?

My head was turning lunatic with all those baffling sights. We crossed our lawn and reached our home. Tim had locked the house from behind so he started unlocking the door. I could see the woods behind our house. They were still dark and silent but so unnatural and deadly now. Something moved behind one of the pine trees; a shadow of someone keeping an eye on us.

"Here Sir, it's done. Let's go inside."

I looked at Tim and then looked back at the shadow but couldn't see any. The tensed face of mine turned pale and the sight of fright could easily be noticed by anyone. Cold sweat drops had appeared over my lips and forehead.

"Did you see that?" I said in a panicked tone while pointing out at thin air towards the woods with a shaking hand.

"See what Sir?"

"That, there… There was somebody standing in the woods. Someone was looking at us," trembling in fear and confusion.

At first Tim tried looking towards the woods to see if he could see anyone. But it was quite dark to make a difference if something was there or not.

"Ah Sir, I am sorry but maybe it's just the darkness of the woods making you see things. The shadow play of the trees might be tricking you. We should get inside. Also Sir we need to look after your injury too."

"But it was right there Tim. I don't know where it went now. Aah… my head is in a lot of pain now. You are right, we should better get inside first."

Tim brought up some cotton and bandages to dress up the wound. The stone might have been quite sharp to have such an impact. It's been just a few days since I got better from the previous injury and now holding on to a new one. How insanely things are running in my life and all credit goes to that letter that was not more than a bad omen for my life.

"Oh that letter! Holy God! Where did I keep it now?"

I panicked as I started searching my pockets since it was with me at noon. I had taken it along for inquiry. Where did it go now? Did I drop it somewhere? I tried looking on the sofa too if it was beside me. There was nothing on the floor either. Alas, it's gone! My Goodness did I drop it near that window? What am I supposed to do now?

Tim could clearly make out by my alarmed face that something had gone terribly wrong with me. But he felt like keeping it unnoticed in order to calm the situation. I was here stuck in perplexity, not knowing what to do next. I had some painkillers for the moment and lay down on the sofa to have some rest. Though, my running mind wasn't allowing me to have peace at all.

Tim went to fetch some tea for me. It was a very gruesome day to survive. I wasn't finding this place beautiful to adore at all anymore. Someone was really after my peace and that's what was haunting me now. How could somebody be so intolerant or insane to make people suffer for no reason? I tried recalling all my foes that I might have had in existence, who could have planned to hurt me. But I believe they would not have been so ruthless. I was completely losing my senses now. Things were getting edgy and unnatural to fit in. I had my eyes closed to relax a bit. My body felt tired and I was still feeling dizzy.

"Nobody lives here, don't you get it!!!" I woke up suddenly by the alarming voice of the old lady with that wrinkled face just falling on me. My goodness, those visions are still haunting me. The whole scenario had turned disturbing and I was feeling restless now.

Tim and I had dinner late that night. I wasn't feeling like going to bed so I thought of returning to my working desk. I had lost the vision I once had when I came here for the first time. My window was open and the forest was the first sight I used to have from my window while writing but it wasn't the same anymore. I closed the window and put on the curtains to pervade the sight. Tim came to see me if I was doing fine. He could clearly see the changes in me and was feeling sorry for it.

A thought struck my mind suddenly as I saw Tim in my room. The newspaper guy, yes he could be a great help for me. I can ask him about that nasty lady and he could even help me get back my letter. My mood has lightened up a bit now. I was relaxed for the moment since I had someone who could help me come out of the dilemma easily. Also he seemed to be doing well with those crazy people in there. He might know a lot about them. But one thing was certain about that house. It had a weird aura that I experienced when I had first entered their premises. They must be into something illegal to hide so much from people outside. Was it some kind of black magic ritual going on there? No, but black magic is just a myth. Or is it? I had seen that shadow hiding in there. Maybe they were hiding some secret, maybe they were the real secret keepers. They must be the ones writing such letters to shove people away. But, what was that shadow in the woods? What was it doing there? Who was it keeping a constant eye on us from there? It must be some act of theirs to make me scared and run off from this place.

Ben must help me to get to the bottom of this conspiracy. I have to keep him on my side first. I need to convince him how torturing this had been for me all these days and how this was harming my mental peace and normal life.

"Tim you need to hear one thing. Just let me know tomorrow whenever Ben comes up with the paper. Ask him to talk to me once."

"Okay Sir. You should rest for the time being Sir. It's very late now."

"Hmm I will just go to sleep now. You can also sleep next to me today. I might ask for something at night."

To be honest that night had been sleepless for me. My mouth was drying a bit and I wanted some water. So I looked around for the bottle but it was empty. I saw Tim lying next to me deep in his sleep and I didn't feel like waking him up. So I took the bottle and went downstairs to fetch something to drink. I went into the kitchen and our window was open. It was a slow breeze outside making the curtains sway with it in its direction. I was closing the wind but to my surprise I saw those nasty people doing something outside their house in the middle of the night in pitch dark. I couldn't make out clearly what they were doing and who they really were. All I could see was a person digging up the lawn in front of their door and the other one standing and observing the act.

"Sir, why didn't you wake me up? Do you want something?"

Startled by the voice I turned back and saw Tim half asleep standing behind me. I looked back at the neighbours but there was no one there now. It's been just a matter of seconds and also the ground didn't seem to have been dug up by someone. My head was turning insane, maybe I was having visions due to the fear that had made home inside my mind. They must be the hallucinations that were trying to play along with my sanity. I didn't want to explain it all to Tim about whatever was happening with me, as he was quite small to understand things and I didn't want him to fear something.

He was a pure soul and he might take it the other way since he is already a believer of such unnatural things you see.

I fetched some water and we went upstairs to our room. I had a sound sleep thereafter with Tim narrating some stories for me to fall asleep. They acted like a lullaby, his sweet voice adding on to the effectiveness.

The stars were twinkling in the sky. The shadow in the woods was gazing at our house, us being unaware of the outer world around us. The raven was now sitting on our rooftop breathing silence on a full moon night.

It was a new day now. Tim brought tea for me on my bed. It seemed quite a refreshing morning and I was desperately waiting for it. I got up to have my tea. It was nine o'clock by now and Ben could be any time in here.

"Tim just keep an eye on the boy. Don't let him go without meeting me. Okay?"

"Okay Sir. Don't worry. I will take care of it definitely."

I had my tea and was getting freshened up for the day. Tim was working for breakfast and then he came up to get my injury dressed up. We then both went downstairs to have our breakfast on the table. The birds were chirping outside. We could see a clear sky today unlike the one we had yesterday. Tim was looking at my eased face and body language and was happy to see me normal again. Though he didn't really know what exactly was going on in my life. We cleaned up the dishes together and cleared the kitchen top and then I sat on the sofa facing the main door. I was looking at the door in excitement and relief waiting for all my answers today. Tim was busy aligning the dishes. I was ready to jump on my feet to open the door for the boy any moment. The clock was ticking disturbing the silence of the scene. I was dying to see the boy in front of my eyes today. My anxious face was popping out its eyes in search of something really important for me. This was quite a few minutes now, maybe an hour. He should have been here by now. What was making him so late today? I looked at the clock and it was ten fifteen now. I started getting furious with each minute passing by. My restlessness started taking over my body. Where was he?

"Where did he go now? He was supposed to be here by nine thirty. It's been over an hour now. How irresponsible for such young kids; not taking their job seriously these days."

Tim could clearly see the frustration in my voice. Unfortunately, he couldn't help me today with this. It was afternoon by now and the boy didn't show up today. This was adding on to my curiosity and fury now. Things were taking time and that was bothering me and my peace; unfortunately, it was concerning Tim too now. I had lost the box and then the letter itself, nothing could be worse than this. My whole day passed in having frantic thoughts running in my mind and that could be clearly seen through my daily activities. And that's how I skipped to another day of anxiety.

Chapter

6

Lost and Found

I was in my room today, holding onto the visions and dilemma that I was facing at the moment. I couldn't even involve Tim in this nor could I even explain my whole scenario to anyone. I was afraid to realise what was real and what just hallucinations were. My writing business was getting affected due to my mind not concentrating even a bit since so many days. I sat down on my writing desk and took out the previous manuscripts of my best sellers. I was missing my inspiration; my interest and these things around were making me lethargic and wasted for no reason. I started scribbling on the paper, a random scribbling to throw off my frustration. My head started aching with thoughts so loud in there that I screamed at the loudest and crumpled the paper and threw it on the wall with aggression. I forced my arms on the table and swept off all the stationary from it onto the ground.

"What do you want me to do? Oh lord!!! Am I going insane?"

I cried resting my head into my arms leaning on the writing table. I was so in confusion to even be normal. My head was crashing with weird thoughts. I paused for a moment and then took a deep breath to calm out the things inside my head. I bent down to pick up the mess I created. My pen had rolled down below my bed. So I leaned down to the floor to see where exactly it was. As I started peeping beneath the bed I saw some paper-like thing lying there. So I took both of them out. It was an envelope. AN ENVELOPE!

"IT'S THE ENVELOPE!!! THE ENVELOPE I WAS LOOKING FOR! HOW DID IT GET IN HERE?"

A sudden joy and confused remarks could be seen clearly through my face. I was excited to see the envelope and now I could explain it to Tim like how someone was messing up with me. I wasn't a lunatic all these days but it actually was happening in real life. I hurried down the stairs to show it to Tim who was busy cleaning up the living area.

"Here Tim, see THIS!" in real excitement.

Tim looked at me with a silent glare. And then took hold of the letter from me to open and read it. I was happy to see that my imaginations weren't imaginations anymore. My excitement was making me jump into the air to enjoy my weird victory. Tim was going through the letter and I was desperately waiting for his approval of all my sufferings. I knew he would understand why I was being so impatient and confused all the time. I was waiting for him to finish and he did even. He was shocked and paused for a moment and looked at me and said-

"WOW!" – In an exciting voice.

ME – "YEAHH, WOW!!" with my eyes getting bigger in excitement and then I paused for a moment to review his reaction.

"WOW?" I left in confusion to understand his excitement. Wasn't he supposed to freak out or something? Wasn't it a thing to worry about? What was that reaction for?

He continued, "You got your favourite publication offer for your work. I am so happy for you. Congratulations Sir."

"WAIT! I got WHAT?"

I couldn't understand a word he said. I was so puzzled to even know if I heard it right in the first place. I took the letter from his hands to see what he was babbling about. I read the whole thing. It was a publication house letter. How? I mean wasn't it supposed to be that threatening letter I was looking for that I had dropped somewhere outside. But what was it doing in my bedroom then? I checked the envelope again and it was the same envelope having no sender's name on it with the same handwriting in it. My face turned pale and I sat down on the couch in a state of defeat. Though the letter inside wasn't matching the one I was expecting but the envelope was exactly the same, I still remember that. What was going around? I felt so shattered and imbecile while unable to understand any of it. Tim could sense the changing emotions in me and then he wanted to confront me and ask if I was hiding something from him. I too wanted to vent out my emotions but wasn't sure if he would understand anything. I didn't want him to be scared but by not letting him know and facing it all alone was actually worsening our bond as well.

"Look there is something I need to tell you. I am not okay to keep it with me only," the confused me spoke up with a fumble.

"What is it Sir, you can let me know. Trust me you will feel better after that," Tim comforted me with his warm words.

I could see his concerned eyes looking at me to get relieved of the entire burden I was carrying in my heart. He knew that I needed him the most at the moment. That pain, that sorrow was reflected on my face every moment like a crystal clear mirror. He too wanted to resonate with my feelings and current situation. So I couldn't just hold it inside me any longer.

"You need to believe me. There is something terribly wrong with the people next door. There is this woman, an old lady and someone accompanying her, they were into something illegal. They even threatened me that my life was in danger through an anonymous letter which I lost that day at their yard," as I continued without taking a pause at all.

"I don't know what they are up to but the letter clearly stated that my life is being threatened, so is my peace since when it first arrived. I really don't know what to do. They fled the place before you arrived. They were there and I am sure they are doing all this to put curtains on their evil deeds," I confounded.

Tim was still just trying to understand what all I said. He was quiet not knowing what to say and what not to say. I knew I had no letter with me to explain the seriousness of the scenario taking place but I knew he would definitely not disbelieve me for sure. I was so baffled at the moment trying to speak out all the possibilities ruling my mind. All Tim could do for me at present was to calm me down a little bit. Also he was not sure enough to give a green signal to all of my assumptions as of now. It was hard explaining everything that wasn't looking as real as it was but that was definitely the need of the hour. So I was done with it today all out of my head and my heart. All I expected was to see a reaction from my little brother now and he did react though.

"That's very scary Sir, I mean I am unable to grab a few things but it really does feel that there can be some kind of conspiracy going on in here. We need to find that out but for that Sir you need to calm down and put your brain at rest. Please," say the worried young man.

It felt as if the little kid was now taking charge to protect my sanity even though he used to be very frantic about such things earlier. Maybe he was trying to ease me and was really acting double his age and mind. That actually impressed me and did work for me at the moment..

It was another day now. I still waited for the newspaper kid to show up today at least. It was the only chance to solve the mystery of that junk letter. We were done with our breakfast and my eyes were keeping a constant check on the wall clock we had. And then we hear the doorbell chime. I got up hastily to check the arrival of my most awaited guest. Tim was observing my rush and anxiety from a distance with an expression of feeling sorry for me. But right now all that mattered was that, the kid I was looking forward to seeing standing at my doorstep. So I opened the door in no time to waste. My eyes were full of fury now.

"Who is it Sir?" asked Tim, still standing at his place.

"I don't know. There is no one outside. Someone is really inviting trouble for himself for sure," replied the angry me.

I was about to close the door when I just saw something on the floor. At first I wasn't really bothered but then I recalled something and was taken aback. I picked it up and went outside to see if anyone was around who could have done it. But to my surprise and adding on to my tensions there wasn't a single human being anywhere to be seen. Now this was becoming a bit ugly and a real worrying situation. I just stared at the box of headpins that I had lost before, that was there right in my hand now, and then I returned indoors closing the door behind me. I was carrying an expression of being exhausted and irritated at the same time and Tim couldn't keep his calm any more. He was unable to bear my restless behaviour, so he thought of giving me a silent treatment, as he too was spending time on his own to ignore my problems for the time being. He now continued with his regular routine though I was now not really sticking to my normal day's behaviour. Days went by and there was no sign of the newspaper boy. I was finding my days horrible enough to survive with my growing curiosity. I was now spending time by just staring at the box, God knows who was playing such games with me that I wasn't enjoying at all. Tim had now started behaving in a very absurd manner; he usually came up with revolting behaviour now. He would retort back angrily whenever I used to have things to say now.

I wanted to confront him at times but he usually kept himself busy to not speak on the topic that was turning me insane and ferocious. He took to both indoor and outdoor business on his own. He was going out shopping for groceries and looking out for the whole house. Things were becoming difficult for him as well. We weren't keeping well for a few days and I was so engrossed in my own world that I almost ignored the young mind of Tim suffering all alone. Our house had turned into a place of silence since we hardly exchanged any words or expressions these days. And one day things turned real bad. We had the ugliest messy argument that I still regret.

It was when on a fine regular evening I got to my room and saw Tim searching for something there. He was very tense and was looking for something hurriedly. I stopped at the doorstep to see what he was up to. It took him a few seconds to realise that there was somebody observing him but till then he had got his eyes on what he was searching for. He turned back to confront me after knowing about my presence too with his one hand at his back hiding something he was holding.

"What are you looking for?" I asked him with a serious look on my face.

"Nothing Sir, I was just cleaning up the mess," as he replied in a low tone.

"Cleaning up the mess in real? And what are you hiding there? Let me see," as I moved forward to catch hold of him.

"Nothing Sir, it's just nothing," as he tried to step backwards trying not to get hold of.

I moved forward only to just grab his arm and reveal what was there. To my surprise he was holding the box of headpins. I was shocked to see that and I gave him a questionable stare. To which he just freed his arm and stood at a distance with an agitated expression on his face.

He then threw the box out of the window since I was just stuck in the thought of why he was looking for it. His move was so quick that I couldn't even react a bit. But as soon as I realised my confused reaction had changed into a furious one now.

"What the hell! Are you crazy? Why did you throw it away? Are you out of your mind?" as I hurried towards the window to locate where the box must have fallen. But I could hardly see anything down there. I was so panicked at the moment that I almost could have jumped down the window too but the voice from behind stopped me and brought me to my senses.

"You are out of your mind. You have lost yourself somewhere. You are not realising how much you are harming yourself," yelled Tim at me with all his emotions almost choking his throat.

I looked back at him with my eyes still open in shock. I couldn't understand for a moment why he was acting like this. He wasn't this way before or was he? What made him yell at me so bad? Why was he calling me the crazy one? Did he not understand what was going around? Yeah, maybe he wasn't aware of any of it. Maybe he was too naïve, too innocent to believe or even understand or adapt to the situation. I was breaking up each day and here Tim was on the other side. I thought we were supposed to be on the same page to hold any kind of notion. He didn't trust me any longer. Yeah, now I got it. He lost his trust in me!! He was questioning what I saw, what I went through all these days. He was questioning my sanity. And I couldn't take it anymore. So I decided to do it today more than ever.

"DON'T YOU TRUST ME? She was there that day too and she lives there. I SAW HER!"

I was so agitated by the fact that I had no proof to let Tim know that things were really going wrong around us. I wasn't able to take it anymore. An anonymous person threatening me through a stupid letter, a missing newspaper boy since the day I was looking for him and those crap people living next door and behaving like lunatics. I was really pissed off and I wanted Tim to at least believe me. But Tim was not convinced by my words at all this time. The person who used to trust me blindly for everything and anything was now not ready to even believe a single word I said. For him, I was stressed out and losing my calm due to something he still was trying to figure out. He was worried for me and he wanted me to realise that there was nothing outside but everything inside my head. How cool could I play it now?

"Tim, you are not knowing what I saw. You don't even know about the letter I wanted you to see that day."

"Sir please calm down."

"Someone is ruining our lives and I believe the people next door have something in there, the answers to all these mishaps."

"I believe you Sir and you need to believe me too. There is nobody living out there."

I gave a weird look. How could he even not listen to me? All I was trying to protect us, him and here he was not at all being on my side.

"Sir, I told you the other day when I met the postmaster. He himself told me that the house has no one living there as of now."

"But he did say there used to be people there a few months back. It was the lady and her autistic son." I exclaimed in declaration.

"But Sir, the lady was in a wheelchair for months and you saw somebody walking right straight at you through the window."

"Yeah, but what if she was okay by that time? Also there is a caretaker living with them."

"Sir, they have not been in the town since we arrived. Why would the postmaster lie?"

Our argument was becoming intense with each declaration we made on each other's statements. Also it was the first time in my life till now that Tim was even having a notion against me and speaking it out loud on my face. We both were not ready to get defeated in stating our facts that we believed in. My voice was becoming loud in between with frustration and resentment but still Tim was ready for all of it today. He was ready to make me accept these stated facts which weren't true to me at all.

"Don't you remember, there used to be clothes hanging outside their house? You saw them right?"

Tim was quiet for a moment but he didn't want me to fall prey to the unreal things.

"That could be someone else doing it for them maybe."

"Yeah Tim that means there are people in there. Don't you get what it means?"

"Fine Sir but please just don't stress yourself out on these things. You need to get this that as of now there is no one living out there."

"Fine Tim, now you are that grown up that you will teach me what to believe and do and what not to. Great."

Tim looked at me and was quiet. Maybe I said something that wasn't the way it came out of my mouth. I made him upset and I didn't even realise it in the heat of the moment. Why did I even say it to him? Tim left the room in silence and I was left in guilt there. Maybe he was right, everything was in my head and it was messing up our lives now. I was letting it mess up with us. I was feeling tightness in my chest due to the guilt I created there. I punched my writing desk to blow off the anger that erupted in me due to my ill mouth. I was in tears, so was Tim, in his room sitting in silence. Maybe I no longer was acting like the person he adored the most. I raised my head and slammed the window in front to close it with force. It was midnight by now. I could see the stars twinkling in the sky outside and then those deadly woods. It all started with that thing, the topic of my story, why on Earth did I even like this place at first go?

I was cribbing and blabbering about all that was the reason for all this and then suddenly something moved down there at a distance. I tried looking harder to focus on what it was. And to my surprise I saw two people dragging something of the size of a body towards the woods. I immediately went down the stairs making noise due to my hurried footsteps that made Tim come out of his room. He saw me running to the main door and leaving the house.

"Where are you going Sir? It's too late. It's dangerous to be there in the dark."

"Just wait in here," while leaving the door wide open.

"I am coming too."

Tim followed me outside while I ran towards the woods. The grass was very tall there leading to the forest. As I got closer, I saw the old lady with that grumpy face and a guy dressed in all black covering his face too, dragging up someone with ropes tied to their arms and body. I knew that something was wrong there and those hooligans were up with something terrible. They were into something illegal and they must be the criminals too as I could see. I yelled out loud to stop them.

"HEY! HEY! YOU… STOP THERE. WHAT ARE YOU DOING? I SAID JUST STOP!"

The two caught sight of me and vanished into the woods leaving behind the body that they had been pulling along. I wasn't able to catch them since I was out of breath as it was after a long run. I looked towards the woods but was hardly able to see them and my knees were shaking due to rapid running. I was panting like an old man holding my knees with my mouth open to take in all the air around. All I was glad about was the evidence left behind. But at least I could show the evidence to Tim and we could save us soon from this horrible place. We could leave this place the next morning since he might not doubt my actions anymore. I was happy and I started laughing with joy and content. I looked back at Tim reaching out to me.

"What happened, Sir? What were you running for?"

"Look I told you those idiots can't fool us anymore. See," pointing my finger out at the ground while my eyes on Tim's face to capture the expressions.

"See what Sir?"

"The body, look it's ... (while looking down) where? WHERE DID IT GO?" bewildered as there was nothing on ground.

"It was here only. They were dragging it. I saw them!" I held Tim's arms to assure him about what I was stating and what I had witnessed. He was still, looking at me in disbelief and concern too but didn't utter a word. He didn't want to hurt me.

"You believe me right. I am not mad to run out like this. You know, right?"

I looked back at the woods baffled completely and started searching everywhere near that spot. Tim too tried to cope up with my beliefs since he didn't want to make me feel unhappy. He too tried to search in the long grass around to see if he could find something to ease my anxiety. I too was searching like a crazy person looking for something desperately. It was quite dark in there to see things clearly but I was in no mood to give up this early. I turned back to see if Tim found something or not.

"Did you find something? It's quite big. It must be anywhere here."

Tim nodded to deny any findings yet. He was silently looking at me.

"What? Don't you say that it's all in my head?"

Tim didn't utter a word. I was just staring at him, waiting for him to speak. And then suddenly I just saw him fall down on his face to the ground and he cried in pain as his face hit a rock down there.

"TIM!!!" my eyes opened wide in utter shock to what just happened.

HE SCREAMED FOR HELP! Something clenched his both legs by the ankles and in a matter of seconds; he was pulled into the woods by some invisible force. Whoosh! HE WAS GONE! I cried out loud his name. I went searching in there but it seemed as if he evaporated into thin air within a matter of seconds for me to even act or react. He was never seen again.

CHAPTER
7

Did You See Him?

I saw him right there. And he was gone. I saw him crying for help and then something pulled him into the woods. All I could sense was him being dragged vigorously by force on the ground and then he vanished. The woods were dark, too deep to even sense how dense it was. Also it was night time and it was already dark to make out things clearly there. I was baffled and numb at the same moment, still figuring out what actually happened. My mind was lost somewhere, not even a thought being in there. I ran madly searching for him into the dark woods. The trees were so tall; their branches were making a roof in there that was disallowing the moonlight to reach the Earth. I could hear the fireflies and some alien insects buzzing at the moment making it totally creepy, noisy and silent at the same moment. If I had never turned towards this side, it would have never happened. I kept walking and calling out his name but there was no response. I was tired now and totally broken in pain. I sat down under a tree and started crying loudly. I tried looking up to the sky that was hidden behind that massive woody umbrella.

I was totally devastated and I felt like killing myself at the moment. My anger and my helplessness were taking over my body and I started throwing stones into the darkness to erupt out my grief. As I moved my hand beside me to grab a stone while sitting on the ground, I felt the stone texture was not as it should be. Something soft but real cold could be felt as I picked it up to see what it was.

My eyeballs almost popped out of my head as I screamed and threw it on the ground. FINGERS!!! They were the fingers of a human! They were so many in number that I didn't realise I was sitting on a pile of them already. I was so in shock that I immediately stood up and ran directly towards my house. I shut all the doors and windows of my house to save myself from all those unholy visions. I went upstairs to my room and hurriedly tried closing the window facing the forest. I could still see a girl standing there draped in a loose white shroud staring right back at me from a distance. I shut the last window. I cried my heart out that day. My brother was taken away and I couldn't even hunt for him right now. Why were the human fingers there? Someone was on the hunt. But who was it and why was this happening? I thought of the criminal backgrounds that family might own. And they must have kidnaped my kid too. I was planning to inform the local sheriff next morning about the crimes taking place in this small town. I needed to save my brother from those butchers. But for now, I had to wait till morning. I didn't sleep that night. Every second seemed an hour for me to even bear.

The visions of Tim disappearing into nowhere were haunting me every now and then. Oh lord, I needed strength to find my brother and save him. I would never ever return to this shitty place in my entire life. I just needed another chance to make it all like it was in the beginning. I would never ever let Tim go away from my eyes. All this was happening because I was crazy justifying things and proving things. Why did I even not listen to my child? He wanted to keep me safe and happy and I just left him in those scary woods. It must be dark in there, how would he even find his way out from there? I couldn't stop the thoughts running madly in my head. I couldn't hold on to my tears anymore. He was there with me and I let him out in danger. How foolish of me to let the kid be out in the dark all alone.

"I AM SORRY TIM! I AM SO SORRY! I AM REALLY SORRY!!!" as I broke down in tears and started slapping myself to punish for the gruesome crime, the unholy crime I committed against my loved one, my life, my only hope.

"I HATE MYSELF FOR LETTING YOU SUFFER! WHERE ARE YOU? OH LORD, PLEASE BRING MY TIM BACK."

I waited for the Sun to rise and then I walked up the hill with a heavy heart to the nearest police station. It was a small dwelling cum office for the local sheriff. There was a lock in there and a notice on the door stating – "BACK AT 9 A.M.! EMERGENCY SERVICE!"

I looked at my watch to see what time it was. The hour needle was still at seven. The birds were flying over me in the clear blue sky. I sat down at the doorstep waiting for the arrival of the sheriff. I was there for around two hours sitting quietly and recalling all the happy moments I had with my little brother. I was exhausted and heartbroken. This place was quite far from our place and it hardly had any neighbours around. Just a few minutes later, a fruit vendor came up next to the station and started setting up his shop. He looked at me and gave an annoyed look and then continued with his business. He was a middle aged guy and seemed to have been in the town for quite a long time. I looked at him and thought of picking up the conversation to enquire about a few things and to pass my time as well. He stared at me in dislike and I did not know the reason behind that look.

"Hey Sir, do you live around here?"

He gave a silent stare again making it clear that he was not interested or in the mood at the moment.

"I mean I don't want to disturb you but can you please tell when the sheriff will be back?"

"It's written over there. You can read it yourself," replied the vendor in a harsh tone, pointing out the notice on the door.

I was quiet now but I wanted to know a few things and it was important for me to gain his attention. So I stood up and looked for the fruits in his stall. I bought a few bananas and oranges to make the vendor a bit comfortable. He was still engrossed in his work, holding on to his character of rude and blunt guy. Maybe that's how his nature was and now I was okay with it so I smiled back at him.

"You live in that old general house, right?" asked the vendor with his eyes set on me.

"Oh, yeah down the slope. How do you know that?" with a surprised look on my face.

"I used to take fruits for the previous owner. He was fond of that place. Why did they even sell it off to someone like you?"

"You said- Someone, like me, what does that even mean? Oh, okay. Well I am just renting there. I don't understand what's wrong with this town."

"The town is full of saints and you are bringing grief and pain to all of us. YOU BETTER GO BACK TO THE PLACE YOU CAME FROM! YOU DEVIL!" yelled the furious vendor and I was taken aback.

I left the stand to take my place at the station doorstep. The vendor was staring at me in fury and revenge. I wasn't able to understand what was wrong with him. I didn't even disrespect him or something to have such an experience like this. His reaction made me hate every human in here. And then I saw a big man in uniform at a distance coming towards me. Oh that was the sheriff. He came and bid 'morning' to the vendor and looked at me. He seemed to be in his late fifties now, and must be approaching his retirement any time soon. He had a pot belly; a round wrinkled face with grey moustache and fine blue eyes and seemed to be of a very jolly nature through his behaviour. He could even be a Santa for a day if needed as he had similar looks.

"Oh, Sir, sorry for making you wait for so long. I had an emergency outside the town," while opening the lock of the station.

I followed him inside and I could see a fine control room having a desk and two chairs with an old cabinet at the corner of the room. There were a few files lying on the table and a pen stand with a classic blue mental cap with antique classic designs on it. I was busy gazing at the beautiful piece of art in admiration, and then I was interrupted by the sheriff's query.

"So, how can I help you Sir?"

"There is a crime going on in this town Sir. YOU NEED TO STOP IT!" as my anxiety took over the place to impose my facts by resting my arms on the desk.

The sheriff was busy writing something on the charge sheet and then he laughed and continued-

"Don't tell me somebody broke your pots in the garden or broke your window pane."

"That's not funny Sir. I am here to report about my missing brother."

The sheriff raised his head to confront me for a second and then continued with his thing.

"Did you say missing? I believe he must be playing some kind of hide and seek with you."

"No Sir, he has been kidnapped and I know the culprits."

"Sorry, you said kidnapping? You need to stop making crazy jokes here. I warn you not to mess up with me. Don't you know? No one can go missing from here. Also there is no crime reported like this from the past 30 years," while closing the file and keeping it aside. I looked at the file and then the sheriff. His calm face was making me agitated now. I was here to complain and he wasn't even interested to know the case.

"Sir, believe me I saw him disappear in the woods. There is this lady, some crazy lady, and her crime partner; they have been wiping out human bodies to the woods. I saw them. You need to come with me."

"I am sorry, what did you say?"

"The woods Sir, they dragged him to the woods and they must have kidnapped my brother too," with a shaky voice and tears in my tears and anxiety taking over my body.

"THE WOODS, you say! Are you the person living in that old house of the General?"

"Yeah, but how does that matter? Please believe me Sir; my brother is in real danger."

The sheriff was giving a firm stare as if I was the culprit to whatever I was stating. It wasn't the reaction

I was expecting from him. Wasn't he supposed to file my case and start up with the investigation? It was a case of abduction and I do believe an immediate action was needed for it to avoid any disaster. Why were the town people so strange, even the police guy. How on Earth would I now find him and save him?

"You are a lunatic. Don't waste my time. Just go home," he bashed at me.

I knew if I stayed there a bit longer he might even put me behind bars. So I left the station and hurried back to my place and said a few terrible things to that vendor outside giving a cold look.

"I am not devil! YOU ALL ARE! BETTER BURN IN HELL!!"

I hurried down the street and saw people giving cold stares as if I was at the wrong place. Good heaven, I couldn't even leave that place without Tim.

It was evening by now, so I decided to catch those butchers red handed since that was the only way to get to Tim. I planned up everything and looked for even an iron rod if needed as a backup or in defending or I could even beat the soul out of them. Also I took the camera with me to capture their heinous work or rituals. They had been the worst nightmare of my life. As it turned dark I took on to my mission of making them repent and undo their evil deeds.

SCENE (INSIDE NEXT DOOR)

I slowly crept into their house from one of the back windows. It was still dark in here with no lights on. I tried making no noise with my backpack on my back, filled with detective stuff in it. No wonder the house seemed empty like Tim had told. I could see a wooden staircase going up in front of the window. That was the exact place from where it all started. I slowly tiptoed to the room next to that place where I had seen the mysterious dim light on that day. But it was dark there today. As I slipped into the room, I saw heavy brown curtains blocking the very minute beam of light from outside. So, I lit up my torch to see the inside view since there was no one on the ground floor at least to notice me. I started looking around to find some clues. But to my surprise the room was a holy gem. The things were shiny and they all seemed to be antique pieces beautifully preserved. The whole room was filled with such precious preserves. As I moved around to every corner of the room, my eyes were star stuck at the jewels present in there. I was still mesmerised from the view, and then something caught my sight. There was a huge painting hung on one of the walls. I turned my torch to see it properly. It had a figure painted on it with a strange black cloth wrapped around the face of the figure. I was so engrossed in that painting that I couldn't move my eyes off the black cloth. I was standing still staring hard at the covered face and then suddenly a liquid-like substance started dripping down the painting from right below the cloth spot. It was red as the colour of a cherry. Slowly and slowly, it covered the whole painting and dripped down onto the floor.

Was it blood? My throat was feeling sweaty and so was my forehead. I wiped up my face with my handkerchief and was about to put it back into my pocket, then I noticed something wrong with it. There was blood on it. I freaked out and almost tripped on something on the floor. I had a terrible fall with my head hitting an old side table. I tried getting up and my torch just fell off my hand and rolled towards the obstacle that made me fall. The light was falling on something, that something was a half cut HUMAN ARM! I Panicked and ran towards the window to escape. The house was a slaughter place as I could clearly see that. I rushed towards the window I came in through but alas it was closed and wasn't even opening no matter how much force I applied. I was now trembling in fear and then I heard footsteps upstairs. I ran back to the room to hide myself. Slowly the footsteps became louder just a wall away. And then I heard a voice scolding someone.

"ENOUGH, CHARLIE! I KNOW WHAT YOU ARE UPTO. You are the one adding sedatives to my drinks every day. You think you can fool us?" said the female voice.

"Oh, dear you think you are smart to find that out? HAHAH! How foolish you are," exclaimed the masculine voice?

"Why are you doing this? I will tell everyone about your deeds," shouted the lady.

Then they started murmuring something and it was hardly audible. I tried eavesdropping through the wall and as I bent forward to hear clearly, I lost my balance and fell on some china dish pot lying next to me. And it broke with a loud sound. I was damn nervous at the moment that I tried running to the other place to hide. The two had already ended their argument or whatever it was. I was trembling in fear of getting caught. I closed my eyes to meet my fate and my heart was pounding out so loud that I could even hear it into my ears. I waited for them to look for me. It was around five minutes but nobody came to check in there. I was still hiding to at least be safe for the minimum time I had. It was quite a time now and there was complete silence. I took courage and got up to escape as soon as possible. I had switched off the torch to not get noticed easily. Though it was becoming difficult for me to find my way through, but I managed to move by staying close to the walls. As I peeped into the next room from where the voices were coming, I saw there wasn't anyone at all. I tried going upstairs now to see what exactly was going on here. There was pitch dark silence in every room and they seemed to be quite filled with dust as I sneezed due to the inhalation. This was so weird and I felt as if the place wasn't really used by anyone for a long time. I turned on my torch since it was already an empty place. My mind was now getting used to the terrible things and creepy scenes happening around. I knew now why the postmaster had said that this place was abandoned. Maybe all that I saw or heard was mere messy confusion of my mind. But, my brother; he was the only reason I couldn't deny a few of the occurrences till now. There was no evidence in there except for the hand that I saw down stairs and now I wasn't even sure if it would be there by now, since things like getting vanished on their own to just prove me insane. But I still went downstairs to check on my luck. Alas it wasn't that great like always. The painting was all right with no signs of any kind of liquid or blood dripping down. The floor was clean with no arm or even a piece of flesh but only dust particles to be swept off someday.

My instincts were working perfectly somehow in some places though. So I started walking out of that antique room and it's then when I stepped on something again but this time of smaller size though. It was almost going to crush under my foot. I picked it up to find that it was just a pen.

"Oh! Thank goodness, not another freaking thing," as I looked at the beautiful antique piece with deep blue colour and sighed with relief. But then the expression just left my face the very same moment and turned into an intense one. It seemed I saw it somewhere before. Wasn't it the same pen that the sheriff owned? Yeah it was exactly the same. But what was it doing here at this place? Was he here before me? Does he know something? But he wasn't even interested in my case at all then why would he even be here? Or was he? I put the pen inside my pocket and then went to the window I came from to see if I could still exit from there. And yes it was open this time and I jumped through it and landed on the ground outside, breathing fresh air. I had to go back to my place to figure out what to do next. I stared at the woods while walking towards my house.

They were the scariest background I could ever have for my house. I just went indoors shutting all thoughts for the time being.

I went upstairs and changed to my nightwear to slip into my bed. I opened the side table drawer and kept the pen inside and tried sleeping thereafter. For today there were no hauntings for the night for the first time. Maybe the dose for today was already over in the house next door. Joking! I know it's not the right scenario to have fun about this serious problem going on in my life, I was better off to sleep. I knew the first person I was supposed to meet in the morning and I was prepared for it now. This whole town seemed like it was filled with idiots and lunatics shoving people away and yes they messed with the wrong person this time. I was not going to leave each one of them for playing such dirty games and snatching my brother from me.

It was next morning now. I got up early and I took a loaf of bread to prepare my dry sandwich. I went upstairs to change and then I was ready to leave. Oh maybe I was forgetting something, THE PEN. I went back to my bedroom and opened the drawer only to find an envelope lying beneath the pen. I took it out to see what it was and to at least read it once before giving any sort of reaction. Yeah same envelope, the lost one but I need to read it to be sure so I went through it and to my surprise this time it really was the one I was looking for. But how did it come here, it wasn't there at night. I looked at the pen and was enrooted in thought and then something struck my mind. I took a paper and started to write with it. You won't believe it was the same ink used in the letter too. Oh I forgot to mention earlier that it was a fountain pen. Though people can have many others too but I was feeling as if it had something to do with the sheriff now. All I wanted and prayed that he should not just disappear like everyone else did before. And even if he does, I need to get to him as soon as possible for real. So I took the envelope too with me.

I went up to the police station to find him but to my surprise I saw the vendor standing at the doorstep with stone in his hands. He was having a fierce look on his face and I stood at a distance to find out what he was up to. He roared at me and started throwing stones he was holding. I was terrified by his insane act and I started saving myself.

"HEY!!! STOP!!! ARE YOU MAD? YOU ARE GOING TO HIT ME!" saving myself by keeping my arms in front to hide my head.

But he didn't stop and increased his speed instead. I was shocked to see that there was not even a lock at the station. Wasn't the sheriff knowing what was going on outside? What kind of people were they? Also such an act was taking place right in front of the law protector. Where on Earth have I landed?

"YOU ARE MAKING US SUFFER. GO AWAY YOU DEVIL!!! JUST RUN OFF FROM HERE! THIS PLACE IS NOT FOR YOU!" yelled the vendor from behind as I started leaving for my home.

"ALRIGHT DO HELL WITH YOUR PLACE!" I replied back while walking.

Everything was turning complicated now. No one seemed to be in a good mental state in this town. And that was worrying me now since they were not letting me find my brother nor were they ready to hear my story.

Chapter
8

She's Hiding-Look!

It was a stormy night today and it's been around a month now. My efforts had all gone in vain and I had no courage left to start up with the hunt again. But I was reluctant to give up on my heart that was still longing for a miracle to happen. I was living a deadly life imprisoned in my own house. The girl in the woods had been giving me visions now and then. I had been lying in my bed looking at the ceiling above. I was completely engrossed in my thoughts during the silent stare. It was raining heavily outside and thundering and sudden flashes made the night look wilder. The lights were already off and I could see the sudden glimpses of the ceiling painted in clear white colour with each flashes of the lightning outside. The dripping sounds of the rainwater from the roof outside the window, was reminding me of the day when I had lost my heart forever. The two significant days impacted my life so hard and were yet so apart. The day when I met that lovely face giving me hope to live my life in a better way and the day I saw it vanish in deep darkness tearing off my heart into pieces of remorse and pain. This wasn't a pain that would go away with time. It was different and suffocating at the same moment. It was something that had killed me from inside, making me a moving lifeless body. I knew I can't give up this early. I knew I won't ever give up this early. I knew he must be alright. He will be alright… he had to be alright. But where was he? I could still hear the scream asking for help but Oh Lord how could I even not be able to help.

Was it the forest that ate him up? Or did it? How could a forest eat somebody? He must have been hungry there. Somebody must have kidnapped him to take revenge from me. But what the poor little soul would have done wrong to anyone to even suffer for no reason.

(THUD… SOUND OF SOMETHING FALLEN ON GROUND)

I snapped awake from my thoughts to find the lights beside my bed but to my surprise there was a power cut due to bad weather. The sound was so loud and clear and it happened to be near the end of my bed. That loudness of the sound had made it appear that something had fallen from a great height.

"What was it?"

I crawled over my quilt to see what it was. As I leapt towards the corner of my bed, I could see some hairy stuff lying on the ground more like the size of a bowling ball. I crept a bit further to have a closer view. It was quite dark to make a difference and know what exactly it was. All of a sudden the lightning flashed at the window and I saw the two white balls like eyes popping off that thing with some hair cap.

It was a human flesh, A FACE, A HEAD, a freshly cut HUMAN HEAD….. TIM!!!

"AAHHH! Holy shit! What was that?" I jumped back to my bed top trembling in fear. There was a head lying down there in my bedroom as I screamed at the top of my voice with my throat muscles almost choking off in fear and the yell was so loud making my veins appear to burst out of my neck. I could feel the cold sweat all over my temple and running down my back making it all wet.

I felt like running towards the door to what I saw a girl around nine or ten, dressed in all white with some stains on her gown having long hair drenched in water, falling over her dress, standing right at the doorstep. She slowly leapt down on the ground and crawled slowly and slowly like a child moving towards my bed. I wanted to break the wall to flee away from the place with my feet frozen and seemed to have embedded into the bedding itself. I tried freeing my legs but they were stuck like being in cement. It was similar like something had clenched it hard enough to even move a bit. I looked back at the girl but there was nothing in sight. I was still struggling with the quilt and trying to move my leg but I strangled further and fell right on the bed facing the bottom corner with my head clinging off the bed.

As I tried raising myself up I saw the girl there sitting on her knees with both hands on the ground and leaping over something beneath her body. I froze again when

I saw it. She was feeding on something and then she stopped!! My gut clenched with numbness and scare as I saw her raising her head slowly with her eyes staring right back at me through the long hair falling on the ground drenched in something making them wet. Her eyes were blood red filled with rage and her stare was like a deadly scavenger ready to tear off my cold dead flesh. The face grinned at me with blood and flesh drooling down its chin. The head was still lying there on the ground half eaten by the girl. It was having maggots on half of the face left barely recognisable. It seemed as if it was there for ages rotten to the core. She started moving towards me with her scary face and mouth covered in blood. My nerves tightened with each movement of hers and I could feel the sweat running along the length of my nose and dripping on the floor. Her face was now an inch away from mine. I could see her white skin having no blood running in its veins. Her face was ruined by deep scars that seem to have become home for maggots and parasites. I couldn't hold on to the fright and the deadly sight as I felt it was all over for me today. I could feel her wet hair touching my face and then I saw her eyes staring into mine as I closed my eyes in defeat.

The thundering sound came up with the lights of the room and it was once again ignited. I opened my eyes for a few seconds to face my fate and to my surprise it was all gone. There was nothing there. It seemed as if the girl and everything just evaporated in thin air. I looked around in my room to notice something irregular but thanks to lord I was saved.

I didn't turn off my lights that whole night.

SCENE 2 (NEXT DAY)

It was midnight again like always. The moon was red, smelting blood through its presence. Like every ritual night, the howling of the night howlers was adding onto the eerie scene of the moment. I could now clearly figure out that something was wrong with the nights. And it's been a long while since I last had a good sleep at night. They were turning more into sleepless ones and seemed to be haunting me till my death. All I wanted was for this nightmare to end but I could not leave without my brother who must be in need of me. He could be in real pain. Also I wanted to not go near the woods because they chanted miseries in there. I had been there thrice to look for my brother but all I found myself trapped in the viscous spell of the woods drowning me in pain and agony. Also there was nobody living in the next door to even enquire about all what was happening, which in itself was a very absurd thing for me to digest till date. The newspaper guy you remember was still missing from the day since I had been waiting for him to resolve the mystery. It seemed as if the forest was engulfing people and no one knew about all that was happening here in this part of the world. No answers to my mails by loved ones and my colleagues. Not even a single message from my publication about my whereabouts. I was missing out on life, a normal life to be precise.

I could hear the breeze swaying my window curtains. I was sitting up on my bed trying to be okay with the posture since lying down never helped me.

I didn't feel like sleeping at night. I looked out of my window. The woods were staring back at me with silent glare. My days were serving me well with horror and anxiety and at times panic attacks too. The outer world was meeting my inner world and it was turning disturbing for me. My idea of supervision was also no more in working and now only I could wait for another day of hope to arrive with new possibilities. Those woods, that letter, alien neighbours, the little ghost and whatever all was happening – were making no sense at all and I had nobody to explain it to me. I wasn't able to get the catch out of it all. All I needed now was someone to confront me and let me know what it was all about.

Next morning, I was woken up by the birds chirping outside my window. I got up to check if everything was alright in my room since I had some obscene visions every night. But like always things were all okay in the mornings and daylights. The most worrying part of those night visions were that now they had become part of my house. The dead girl had entered my premises and that was giving me chills every now and then. But what were those scenes pointing at? I was unable to follow if it was all the game of my thoughts or some creepy cult practice trying to overshadow their deeds. Something weird and creepy was happening to me which was completely out of my control. I was just worried about Tim since these people seemed to be very powerful and insane at the same time. Also every town person seemed to have been actively participating in making my life a living hell. But I didn't want to surrender to them.

I now thought of fixing some cameras at the end of the lawn to see if I could catch a single movement of those alien powers possessing those people and making them do horrible things. So I went to the market to get some supervision cameras for myself. Though it was a great struggle to pass through furious townies, I somehow managed to get what I was looking for. Now was the turn of installation without being suspected by anyone around. So I carefully planted them in hideous places to be noticed by anyone. Also I had one placed in my ground floor, giving the view of almost the kitchen, the doorway, and the sitting area itself. And it was time to let it work for me now. So I went indoors to set up my laptop for the captures and videos viewing. I was almost finished with my work when I heard someone walking inside my house downstairs. At first I was quiet for some time to hear the noise more clearly, but when I was sure that there was somebody in there; I looked for the footage in the laptop to see who it was since it was an uninvited arrival or some intruder for sure. As I looked into the video, all I could see was an open main door which was probably closed when I first came in. There was nobody seen opening it. Yes, you read it right, the footage showed an empty air opening up the main door on its own which could be quite possible if it wasn't latched probably. But for the sound of footsteps, they needed some explanation for sure. And I was definitely running out of logic now and even words to express what it really was looking like. Although it was daytime and usually such unusual things weren't expected for this time period, you never know how exactly it works. All I could do at the moment was to check myself by going downstairs and that required a lot of courage and strength. So I just left my seat to hold up to my faith and slowly moved towards the door while leaving the laptop open behind. The screen was getting glitches with every step I took towards the door and I was totally unaware about the same. As I reached the staircase, the screen boomed and it was completely blackout with nothing displaying on it. While there, my fear was taking its roots in my heart and mind, with cold sweats running down my temple. All I wished and prayed at the moment was to see something real and less scary and life threatening. I slowly walked down the creaky wooden stairs trying not to make much noise but obviously the floor too was working against my will.

As I reached the ground floor, I saw someone sitting on my couch. At first I stopped at a distance to understand what my eyes were looking at, but then I needed to have a closer look to see what and who it really was. I gathered all my strength to pull up a little closer and suddenly I was stunned to believe my eyes, while my body fell off on its back in shock and fear. There was this lady, a woman sitting on the couch and let me tell you she wasn't a regular woman to speak about. She was different, different to describe in words, someone who you would never want to visit you in real life. She was having a somewhat weird appearance of a distorted face looking more like a burnt corpse. Her eyes were as hollow as an egg shell or a deep dark well. She was silently glaring at my frightened face to suck life out of me. All I could do was to continue the stare game with my shivering body giving no hope of escaping the sight. My body was almost jammed in fear to even move an inch further. She seemed to captivate my soul and my mind and I couldn't help myself from getting close to her now. I was slowly walking on my knees towards the deadly phantom while my eyes still stuck at those hollow eyeball sockets. It was more like a hypnosis trick that was definitely working so smoothly on me. I saw her calling for me like a dead angel in disguise, and with each step the force seemed unbreakable pulling me into her hollow yet burnt arms. I was almost into her arena when suddenly the spell broke by a purring sound. It felt like coming into senses with my head feeling so heavy now and then. What I saw was a black cat sitting in front of me an inch away. It walked off the couch and left the house with its green eyes staring at me consistently.

What? A Cat! No, there was meant to be something else sitting in its place. I knew what I saw and now my mind wasn't willing to accept the changes in the scenes that it had captured. My body was still numb and the feeling of perplexity was floating all over the space. I then hurried upstairs to find the footage to clarify my doubts but all I could find was a black screen making my life a more miserable and feared one. I tried my level best till now but it was all giving me headaches with no results at all. Only if Tim would have been here to witness all what was happening and help me out to differentiate between what needed to be there and what not to be.

I needed some rest for now since things weren't getting any easier and my fear was turning into pain of discomfort and non-acceptance of all the incidents that took place around. This was more like being caught in a situation not knowing which way to move. There was nobody to support me and to help me get out of this situation and state. Only if I could get back to my brother, things would not have been welcomed by me by staying here any longer. But my fate and destiny was not willing to give up on me. It was looking as if everything was meant to just tear me apart – my heart first and now my head. I managed to make some dinner for myself hoping for no surprises walking up to me by the eerie environment around. I had my meal and then went to my room upstairs to feed my body to my bed for a holy nap.

SCENE – 3(ANOTHER DAY-VILLAGER ACTING CRAZY)

Like every midnight, the woods had something to show me. My window was turning into a horror show TV as I looked through it to see those shady woods. Everything had become disturbing for me. Everyone was after my life; the ghost of a little girl scaring the life out of me, the crazy mysterious neighbours slaughtering humans and no one even knowing or caring about the missing people, and the folks around trying to blame me for every incident taking place in the town. And the most important person, that mad vendor ready to tear off my flesh and have a feast with it someday. He was the most important because I knew he wasn't scaring me but actually trying to kill me in real life. Also that Sherriff was being of no use in this town.

Believe me, they all were nuts that one day a boy in the town started throwing eggs at me and instead of stopping her kid; his mother joined him too and started reviling for no reason. And one of the ladies in the town accused me of giving her nightmares which were quite funny and weird for me to hear or even digest. The florist had put allegations on me for his son getting injured in an accident which I had nothing to do with. I didn't even know the guy. Also I was meeting them all for the first time and I wanted it to be the last for me. They all had so much hatred for me but I had the double of it for the whole town. They just ate up my happiness and were now backlashing me instead of helping me in my loss. This had to be a story to tell the rest of the world how cruel mankind can be to one of its own kinds.

Things turned worse when I came to know that the town had boycotted me completely, my power being cut permanently till I recede from here. I was in utter shock to even react to this inhumane act of theirs. At first I thought there must be a mistake or bill pending but it was all cleared. Also they cut off my water supply too, making my life a real hell. But they never acted like this when Tim was around and now when he is gone they seem to shed off their fake skins. It was one morning that I saw some kids outside my house drawing something on the walls. I shoved them off to see "THE DEVIL" written on it. Someone had scribbled –"GO BACK" too. I was now feeling like killing each one of them. Also I tried making a call to my landlord but he was unavailable.

The nights were already haunting ones; not letting me sleep for a moment and now thanks to the town that my days were also turning into nightmares. I had already closed my writing business days back or else it would have been the best seller plot if I wrote it down. You see how life is, I wanted inspiration and now I had no confidence left in there to even write a single word. And how could I even write one when my brother who helped me in my stories by being just beside me wasn't there anymore. I did not know what to do next.

It was afternoon and I went to the kitchen to see if I had something to eat. But everything was finished there. I found a stale bread loaf in the refrigerator which I wasn't going to eat anyway. So I rushed back to take my wallet and leave for the vegetable stall up the street. I wasn't already hoping to be treated well by the vegetable vendors since nobody really had a word of respect for me in the town.

As I walked through the street I could clearly see the hatred in the eyes of the people moving around. But I wasn't afraid of anything as of now since I wasn't committing a crime or something. I saw an elderly man sitting on the side of the street with vegetables in his stall. He seemed quite poor since I could see his torn shirt that he was wearing. His clothes were very filthy and I could see very few customers at his shop. I walked straight away to him with all the courage I was left with.

"Sir, can you get me some tomatoes and onions," with a nervous voice.

The vegetable vendor looked up and paused for a second. I was ready for his cussing as well if he wished to but he turned out to be a nice guy. He smiled and said –

"Sure Sir, how much you want."

I was surprised as well as happy by his gesture so I told him what was on my list. Maybe he didn't know who I was because he didn't behave like others. Or maybe he was the only person with brains. I took some fruits too since he was having plenty of them too.

"Thank you," while paying him off.

"Sir, you live near the woods right?" asked the old man.

I was quiet for some time as I didn't want to ruin the happy vibe we shared until his query arrived. I was about to clarify something and open my mouth but he interrupted and said-

"I know you Sir. Don't worry I won't shove you off. I know you are having a hard time at this place."

I was shocked that he had a smile on his face while addressing me. This made me happy after so long that somebody had a word with me, that too a friendly one. I smiled back.

"You don't worry, they are not harmful. They just want to scare you," he continued.

"Yeah but you are different. You don't want to call me a devil unlike others?" spoke of my curiosity.

"Why would I, Sir? They don't know what they are doing. Forgive them. Anyways have a good day Sir."

I bid him goodbye and took the veggies and was off to the street when he said something from behind.

"Don't go near the woods Sir. It won't forgive you."

I turned back with an expressionless face. I stood there still for a second or two to know what he meant. But then a lady came to the stall and started giving me that firm look like everybody. I didn't want to create a scene out of it, so I left.

I was happy that at least I can share my woes with someone who can listen to me. Maybe he can be of great help to know what these folks were up to. I reached home only to find my kitchen window pane broken. Someone had thrown a stone on it. It must be the kids that were strolling around in the noon. I thought of fixing it later. I went straight to the kitchen to cook an immediate meal as I was very hungry by this time. As I was having my meal, my mind was not ready to enjoy it. My Tim too would be hungry. What if they weren't feeding him enough? Or were they even feeding him at all?

After my meal I went to fetch some water from the stream nearby the neighbour's house. Although it was always like taking life in hands whenever I used to be in their curtilage, but one thing was certain by now that there were rarely any supernatural surprises for me during the daylight unlike the burnt lady one. I had to fill two to three buckets of water every day in order to sustain the whole day.

All I had to do now was to talk to that old vegetable vendor whenever I meet him next. For me I was planning to make it happen the very next day. He could help me search my brother as well and he could even save me from all those crazy villagers. Maybe he was also mistreated by them and that's why he isn't like them at all. But he too was talking about the woods. Maybe he knows more than I can even imagine. He was my only hope now.

It was night time. The crickets were making noise outside. I couldn't turn my lights on due to a connection cut so I had prepared my dinner beforehand only in the evening. I had my dinner and I tried sleeping without light that night though I was afraid of the dark nowadays. But I couldn't help myself. I was in my bed now. I had let the curtains open so that moonlight could make a difference. Slowly my eyes got heavy and I slept.

It was 3 a.m. now. My bed felt sudden jerks as if an earthquake had hit. At first I thought it must have been the quake only since everything in the room was shaking, increasing rapidly in speed. I ran out of the house to mark myself safe in case it was a quake. I was in my lawn now waiting for some time to feel safe enough to move inside. It was quite stable by now and it was chilling outside. So I went back to find that my door was stuck. I tried pulling with force but it was locked from inside. I tried moving through the window but it was closed too and then I saw its broken glass pane which I was already supposed to fix anyway. But right now it helped me to open the latch from inside while making my way into the house again. I was just climbing up the window struggling to jump inside but something froze me. My face was having sweat drops taking its surface all over. My eyes opened wide and my vision fixed towards the sink. The white gown girl was standing near the sink holding on to the hair of a boy knelt down on ground. She was holding a sharp knife in her other hand and then she slit the throat of that boy, beheading him, a shower of blood pouring on the ground. And then she dropped his head on the floor.

"TIM!!!"My eyes opened wide as I woke up with a scream. It was morning by now. Thank goodness it was just a nightmare. My back was wet with sweat making the bed damp. I came out of my bed and went downstairs to check if everything was alright. And yes everything was in place except for one thing. There was something fallen on the floor as I bent to pick it up. It was a KITCHEN KNIFE.

Did something happen in real life or maybe I have started overthinking? What if it was a bad omen? I wish it was just a nightmare. I need to find him soon.

My Dear Noble Host

It was now time to go on my mission. The mission was to get to the root of everything. I knew if I met that humble old man openly, people around wouldn't support that. Also I didn't want him to even suffer a bit because of me as I knew they all had problems with me and might even punish him for letting me know the things or their bloody secret. So I decided to follow him to his house secretly and sneak in whenever possible without getting noticed.

I was ready for the day. So I had my breakfast early and took the pen and the letter along to solve this disturbing mystery. My profession was now turning into more like a detective one rather than being an author. Also I made sure I had a picture of my brother too so that I could even enquire if he saw him anywhere in recent days. Now I headed towards the marketplace to see if the old man had been there or not by now. I didn't see him on the spot he was at on the previous day. Maybe I was quite early so I thought of sitting somewhere and waiting. But you know how things were with people here; I had to struggle to find a place to sit in peace. And then I saw the old man at a distance dragging his wheeler cart filled with veggies heading towards his setting spot. I let him set up the stall first and then went to him acting as if I needed some fruits.

"Oh! Good morning Sir. How have you been?" greeted the happy old man.

"Good morning Sir. I am quite well like how I left yesterday. What about you?" in an energetic voice.

"I am fine Sir. Here I have fresh fruits for you. Also if you need I can deliver to your place too since we are up for home delivery. But as you know the scenario here, I might have to be very careful," said the old guy.

"No, no, that's totally fine. I prefer to walk to the market since it's good exercise for sound health, you know."

"Yeah, right Sir," smiled the old man while packing up fruits for me.

"By the way, may I know your name Sir? I mean we can catch up for some refreshing conversations or for some coffee any soon," me in a giggling voice.

"It's Anthony Sir. People call me by the name of Tony. You can use that."

"Very well Mr Tony, will meet up soon then. Thank you for the fruits," as I left smiling.

I knew I couldn't have a long conversation with him since there was danger everywhere for me and it could be for him too. So I went to a park nearby from where Mr Tony was quite visible and sat there for hours. He might go on a break and he even did and I was rejoiced to see that. So before following his trail, I looked around to see if anyone was noticing me or not. When I felt safe, I took on the mission to follow him while acting as if I was just strolling down the street. For God's grace, the streets were not very crowded and people were busy with their own business. I felt like God too wanted to be on my side in this. Maybe he couldn't take it anymore given how much I was suffering. Whatever the reason, I was happy to get along unobstructed by anyone or anything. Mr Tony didn't even have the slightest idea of being followed by somebody and all credit goes to my new developing skills of detective.

Mr Tony seemed to have been living at the other end of the town and that could be the reason why he wasn't much influenced by other folks. He now stopped in front of a very small house, looking very old and ready to fall off in any minute. I saw him open the door and he went indoors. I then looked around to see if anyone was there but the street was empty so I immediately made a move and knocked at the old wooden door. Within a few minutes, the door opened.

"Oh Sir, how come you are here? Come inside please," as he welcomed me into his small world. He was surprised but he was happy at the same moment to see me there. As I entered, I saw a small living area with pretty cute things placed at every corner. It was a cute little world with a tiny kitchen at the backside and a small room attached next to it. It was enough for a single person to stay. I saw a photo frame of a middle aged lady kept on an old side table. I was just looking at it when Mr Tony interrupted-

"That's my daughter. Here, please have it Sir. Please make yourself comfortable Sir," while offering a glass of water.

"She is very beautiful. So she lives with you?" as I asked while drinking the water.

"She lived down the street Sir. She was married to a rich guy in the town. She is no more. I just happen to live with my granddaughter now," while looking at the frame.

"Oh… I am so sorry Mr Tony. That's a sad thing to happen. Sorry for…" I hesitated a bit, not knowing how to console the old man.

"Oh that's okay Sir. Things happen and that's why we call it 'LIFE'," said Mr Tony in a low contended voice.

I was quiet for some time since that made me remember my misery. I knew what loss means and the never ending pain that doesn't let you live your life. You suffocate to the core with a heavy guilt and remorse filled in your heart. You try to break through the thoughts but they haunt you every moment making you feel like ending your life. A LOSS CAN NEVER BE DEFINED THROUGH TEARS OR ANY SORT OF EMOTIONS. THE GUILT OF MAKING THINGS HAPPEN MAKES YOU FRAGILE FROM INSIDE. I knew exactly how helplessness one feels at this moment but I didn't want to rub on his wounds again. He was a nice person. I loved seeing him smile every moment.

"Sir, I got you some tea. I am sorry I wasn't having coffee at home so," while moving the tray towards me.

"I am good with tea. Don't be so formal Mr Tony," as I smiled at him.

I became pretty good friends with him as time passed and as the conversations lengthened. I wanted to win his confidence to help him reveal the story of the woods and the town itself. Since there was no one around, it was the best place to discuss such a sensitive topic with him. Also he could help me with the whereabouts of those criminals hiding next door.

"Mr Tony, I need your help," as I held his hands, with my eyes reflecting expectations.

"What help Sir? Tell me, I will try if I can," said the generous old man.

"Mr. Tony, as you already know, I am having so many troubles in this town. I just lost my little brother too in finding out what grudges people are holding against me. I don't know if you understand, I need to find my brother and I need your help," my eyes filled with tears.

"Oh! Well Sir, I didn't know that. I mean your brother, what exactly happened?" the old man asked with intense concern.

At first I felt like losing hope since his expressions seemed to be of an unaware person. But then I recollected all those moments with my brother and came back with my queries.

"I don't know what just happened with him and I am still figuring it out. I don't know what to do but he vanished into the woods and it's been a few days now and I don't know about his whereabouts…" my throat choked through emotions and tears rolling down my cheeks. Mr tony was quiet and he too had a feeling of distress now reflected on his face.

"I understand your pain. I will tell you one thing. I know that this town…" he was just continuing when he heard his granddaughter screaming inside the room.

"Ah, excuse me please Sir, she is not well actually," as his expression changed to sudden concern.

"Yeah, sure, we can continue later," as I didn't want him to get bothered by me much.

The old man went inside the room, closing the door behind. The child was still screaming, I don't know for what reason and I didn't even ask him before about her health. He then came outside and went to the kitchen to prepare some kind of fast meal while me sitting in the living area waiting for him to finish off with his chore. I was looking at the old racks in there with dust on it. His life was busy but still he was looking after his granddaughter so well and I could sense it through his actions. There were some soft toys lying on one of the shelves of the cabinet. Mr Tony had finished his cooking business and took it in a bowl for the girl inside. I was busy looking at the things kept there and then a strange toy caught my attention. I didn't know what exactly it was so I walked to the cabinet to see the toy closely. It seemed like some sensory thing but quite fascinating and eye-catching. The child was quiet now and I was glad how good understanding he had with her. I was busy trying to figure out how it worked and then I walked slowly towards the half open room to see the grandfather's love for his grandchild. I smiled while I saw the affection and bond between the two. He was feeding his granddaughter with so much patience and care. But something stopped me for a moment and I lost my smile, while my expression changed into a shocked one. The girl seemed so familiar to me with long black hair and that face that I could never forget. She stopped eating and then raised her head and looked at me. IT WAS HER! It was the girl from the woods! I was numb for a moment and shocked when suddenly the toy fell off my hand making a strange noise while hitting the ground. The old man turned around to see who was at the door but till then I had already left the house. He came to the living area to check on me but I wasn't there, leaving him worried now. I couldn't understand the scene I witnessed as I rushed with a heavy heart and I felt like a fool at the moment. Was he the whole time? That's why he was nice to me. He and his granddaughter must be the one's scaring me all these days. May he was one of them helping others to shove me off from the town. I was heartbroken and confused. Also a feeling of being scared was also there. They all were mad. They all were living with a deadly ghost and haunting me with their tricks or whatever that girl was.

While walking back down the street, I felt someone was keeping an eye on me but my feet continued moving with greater pace now. Things were getting clear but I wasn't sure if they were exactly what was running in my mind. I had a doubt that they were controlling a ghost child. Yeah she was a ghost child with that white gown, long hair, that scary face and that pale skin of hers making it clear that something was terribly wrong with her. Her flesh didn't seem to be of a human. How would they even do that? But I just saw that old guy feeding that ghost. He was with the town people. He too was hiding a secret. They all are hiding a secret. A SECRET UNKNOWN!!! There has to be an end to this, to all of this as soon as possible.

I was sitting on my bed now in my house back again thinking about all the terrible weird possibilities that could come to my mind. What a horrible place it was, filled with scavengers and demons and not even human-like species. But WAIT! WAS THE GIRL THE SECRET!! NAAH! That could be the weirdest thing to even to be protected by someone. He said it was his granddaughter and she was sick. Maybe that's what he meant. But he was a good guy. Wasn't he? He was the whole damn time the only sane person I came across. And He was about to tell me something. HOLY SHIT! HE WAS ABOUT TO TELL SOMETHING!

"OH God! I am such a fool to run away like this. What if he had something important for me?"

I bellowed in pain and guilt of not hearing the whole thing, while punching the mattress in rage.

I wasted my whole day now. He might not even entertain me now onwards. But that girl was right there sitting next to him. I still remember the visuals of her haunting me every night and she was the same ghost, a living nightmare. But he was so relaxed sitting there. He cooked for her. Maybe I hallucinated again. I don't even now understand the difference between reality and hallucinations anymore. My mind now homes the worst visuals and now every corner of this place gives me Goosebumps and chills. I never knew that my stories do have existence somewhere stating facts and building reality. My Tim was right; YOU NEVER KNOW WHAT'S OUT THERE IN THE WORLD WAITING FOR YOU! I pity myself for making fun of my kid that time. He wasn't naïve but I was foolish to mess up with the wrong things. And he ended up being a scapegoat for the things I did. I wish I could just hug him once and say how much I miss him, how much I loved him.

Being an author I now realised what an art of writing is and believing in it means. Not everything or anything is for fun, like these people mocking me now. But now this has turned into a real fight against the evil and the darkness it brought to my life. I now had to let all the demons suffer to let the brightness take over the world again. No matter how hard it would be, I need to get back to Tony to know the real story and I am ready to face it now.

It was midnight by now and I had missed my dinner for today. Also without lights I could hardly work in the kitchen properly. Nor would I take chances with that unholy thing that loves to wander in my house as if it's hers. She was a WALKING DEAD OMEN! Yeah she was and it's always her who managed to appear in any corner of the town and at any time. This Ghost was giving me real pain in the ass as well as head. Also I often had the thought of chopping off all the trees in the woods to eliminate the deadly scary omens they home or create. But I couldn't do that otherwise they all will get exposed and they, might even chop off my head. Also this place is so far off from the city and in the outskirts that nobody would ever come to know what exactly happened to me. While you see not even a friend or colleague of mine or even the publisher is concerned to connect with me till now, so you can easily know how much they even care. And not forgetting my landlord missing. How did he even happen to live at a place like this before? Or maybe he too disliked it and left for the city instead. There is no chance of surviving in here for too long. Either they will kill you or you will kill them. And there can be just brutal slaughtering around. I don't understand how they even weren't scared of the Almighty. Also I noticed something wrong with the houses along the street. There seemed to be a pungent eerie smell floating in the air everything I passed through it. Even when I entered Tony's house, the similar smell came out of his room that day. That smell was so common here even it used to be there in my house sometimes and seemed to be coming from the woods side. I though couldn't guess from where it was. I felt like every person in the town was hiding some mystery in their homes. Basically for me they were into some kind of illegal cult practice and this needed the attention of rest of the world. Since this had made them crazy not having any emotion of kindness, generosity, or love. Also the policeman, he was not even a real police guy. I needed to report him as well but what if he was good with higher officials, I might end up in trouble. God knows who else was involved in this whole mess.

I knew that I needed to see Tony again in fact frequently to get out of this as soon as possible. I need to get to his place again without letting anyone know in the town. I dozed off that night with all the imaginations and self-talk ruling my brain. I was fortunate enough to spend a normal night sleeping that day. Tomorrow was going to be a tough day again. I wish God Blesses ME and not them instead. Let's just end this now. GOODNIGHT!

Once Upon a Time When

"You really want to know it?" the old man asked, with a concerned yet firm voice.

"Yeah and that's why I am back. Look, I am sorry for being so rude that day. I was just terrified," hesitating a bit.

"Hmm, I saw that. That's fine but you can't be here for long. There are people around and they don't like seeing you here. I hope you get that," while he asked me to sit down. We both sat in that cosy little living area of his as he started narrating the scene-

"It all starts long back from the day we all were happily living in the town." It was the best place on Earth according to many people who came across as tourists or just visitors since they loved and enjoyed the hospitality by the locals. This town was named Viva City, meaning happiness as it had the best people in the state. The town was small but beautiful at the same time preserving the nature around as well. Everyone here loved each other, supported each other and even the living creatures around. For them 'LOVE CURED DISEASES'; here disease was not always clinical but at times emotional too. Therefore, by God's grace everyone had a sound and healthy life. The folks had festivals and carnivals every month to celebrate the essence of the town. I was quite young at that time living with my parents down the street and later shifted here when they died. We were a happy family; the entire town was a family. We often used to have dinners together, sometimes at friends or relatives place or at times mass dinners. It was more like a Met Gala thing, everyone coming up with amusing attires and partying together. Life was easy and pretty at that time.

My parents were a happy couple and we made a perfect family, living our life to the best we could. Everything in the town was going great. It soon turned into a tourist place. Almost half of the folks including us started renting out to visitors to show them the real world here. And to their astonishment, not even a single penny was charged from them for staying in our houses. Many of the visitors were happy about that and they used to return frequently to our land bringing some more visitors with them. And our town welcomed them with open arms and open hearts. Some of them became our friends too with time.

It was once a visitor named Joseph mistakenly entered our town. He was just an explorer going with the flow of winds. He never knew that this part of the state ever existed before he visited here. It was always random tourists coming up here since we never marketed tourism over here. Nor did we have an idea of the tourism industry growing outside our little world.

Soon Joseph started interacting with everyone in the town. He stayed in one of the houses in the street and he grew fond of the place and people here. He had almost made everyone his friend. Also he was a very smart guy with a wide smile on his face. We actually met at one of the carnivals and then we almost hung around me guiding him through the town, narrating stories and a lot more stuff.

We enjoyed each other's company and he was a funny guy to go out with. We used to have horse rides, fishing together and almost crashing every dinner night with him performing for the town and me supporting him. He almost became everyone's favourite by then. But he had questions for us all. He loved us but he didn't understand why we worked like that. He felt that we were too naïve and anyone could take advantage of that in future. But we had no reasons - No REASONS TO BE THAT WAY- WE HAVE NO REASONS TO BE HAPPY SINCE WE WERE HAPPY! And probably that was the best thing about the town people; contended and with no guilt just smiling our hearts out. He would never force us to change ourselves but he used to suggest things and ideas others could adopt to make our place better with time. Though we were satisfied with what we had, we never felt like changing a thing or two, maybe that's what made us happy- HAPPY BEING WHAT WE WERE! And one day he was off for his journey. I was a bit sentimental at that time but I was happy to make a new friend like him. He bid bye to everyone and we wanted him to visit again soon and more frequently. He was glad to have met us all. Joseph being Joseph a funny guy making all of us laugh during his departure.

Months passed by, and we welcomed new people with time. All glad and excited to happily stay for free here. But I was waiting for Joseph to visit us again. I even wrote a letter to him, asking about his adventures and whereabouts, discussing about life here of the townies and at last told him how much we all missed him and we all wanted to see him again. I waited for his answer but it has been months now since I sent my letter. I thought maybe that wouldn't have reached him yet. That wait was causing a weird type of feeling in me- restlessness and worry that I had never experienced before while being a Vivaian. This was all new for me since we actually never waited for anyone and that's how things were equal for every visitor. I didn't discuss this with my father since I thought it was all wrong to have a feeling like this. We Vivaians weren't supposed to be worried, restless, or even sad since that's how our town spirit never died."

"What does it mean by town spirit? How would that break the town spirit? Isn't it alright to be emotional at times?" my curiosity questioned while being so madly engrossed in the story. This story was growing interesting and filled with so many queries. But maybe it was good not to interrupt the teller so I kept quiet.

"Yeah it was the town spirit, the town spirit which means the spirit of being lively and sound." For us emotions had only two names - HAPPINESS & ... Happiness.

We never had experienced misery in our lives since we had no guilt, no wants, no non-satisfaction, no revenge feeling, no jealousy, and no remorse. Also this was all because we had our nature with us - THE WOODS. It gave us plenty to eat, fresh air to breathe and a lot of resources to make our lives easy and comfortable. Also it gave us the most precious gift of good mental health. SO IT WAS OUR TOWN SPIRIT! We used to worship it like our God, giver, and father. Everyone respected nature and nature loved us back with the wonderful world we had. "

"So why did you say the other day that the woods are dark? Aren't they your God now?" Interrupting confused me.

"Yes they are. They still are. And I am telling you the reason why everyone hates you here. Also why did I call those woods dark? I have your answers but you need to be patient enough to understand how it works."

"Fine, sorry, you continue please."

"So, where were we?" Yeah, the woods those were and still are considered as the town spirit by the townies. People used to go there and celebrate every happy moment of their lives with the woods. They used to leave their goodies and sweets and presents there for the Forest God to accept and in return their lives were filled with everlasting joys. My parents too went to the woods to pray at times and they used to believe that we all were happy because the TOWN SPIRIT was amused and happy.

Time passed by and one day, I saw a man coming with some of his fellows towards the town. He was at a distance but I could still make out who it was through the walk he owned. Yeah! That was my long gone friend - JOSEPH. I ran to greet him and met all his friends too. And then he introduced me to them and we all were happy to see each other. In the group was a girl, quite outspoken and enthusiastic though. She was his cousin. I was quite hesitant to interact with her much but her presence was kind of very attractive. Then Joseph told me that how he liked the town and told to his buddies about it and they all wanted to drop in here at once. So they all landed up together. He then met all the townies and greeted them all. Everyone was happy to see the funny guy again. They all stayed at my place including Joseph, his cousin and two other girls. While the rest two boys stayed in the neighbouring house. Although we all had dinner together, the stays were for the nights only.

The girls used to usually help out my mother in preparing food and we all enjoyed our nights talking out stories to each other. The new people were amazed to see the town so happy and lively and our stories seemed weird for them because they always were happy only - the beginnings, the climax, the end - everything was positive and this made them so interested in our lives.

The most curious out of the group was Joseph's cousin. Her name was Mary. She wanted to know everything and everyone since she said she never lives so happy at her place and she was surprised to see the parallel world in here. She said, the outer world was full of misery and she wanted to know how come they still were so untouched by the outer materialistic distractions. I used to explain to her how we believed in things here. She started spending time with me asking questions and about the town. Me as a Vivaian, used to tell everything pleasantly and gently since we never got agitated or irritated by any questions put at our existence and beliefs. Ultimately she started liking me for being so patient and kind to let her queries get answered with no hesitations and no regrets. Somewhere inside me too was developing a feeling of attraction for the lady since we first met? Mary was a fine woman with her own ideology and ethics and her own beliefs which I appreciated and never felt like correcting since they weren't not so similar like ours.

They all stayed there for two months and then it was time for them to go back. I didn't want them to leave and especially Mary this time. Something made me worried and sad at the moment which was wrong for the Vivaian to experience. We hadn't had our confession yet. Mary was sad too and she wasn't able to express herself as she left. Maybe she wasn't suitable for me. So they left in no time and we all were back with our things. I had started thinking about the time we spent together going out and how curious she used to be about everything and anything. I loved her questions since that gave me a feeling of being interested in. But till then I didn't know if there was any possibility for us to meet again. I wasn't aware about the mutual feeling she had for me till then. So I never had the courage to tell her even when she was here. Days passed by and the feeling of longing and memories made me sad now. I wasn't able to get what I wanted as of now. This made me depressed. I used to sit alone in my room looking out of the window to see if I could see them returning back anyhow. But all I got was days and months and years of disappointment. My parents got worried about my changed behaviour and this eventually worsened our home spirit. My mother went to the woods with presents to ask for happiness in my life.

And one day we had visitors. There was a knock at the door. And I heard my mother rejoice and call out the name I was looking for. 'Mary' she was back. Her prayer worked. I was happy to see her and my parents immediately understood what was wrong with their son. So they welcomed the lady and we all had a great chit chat at the dining table eating our meal and laughing our hearts out again. I experienced the most pleasant feeling that has stuck me since ages. It seemed as if I was just happy till now but I felt overjoyed and lively for the first time. I wanted Mary to know how I felt but I was a bit nervous to hold any kind of rejection. Also the other side Mary was back to confess something. I was scared to initiate and so was she. We just enjoyed hanging out together and soon the town also loved her arrival. She hadn't changed a bit; she was the same, curious, and outspoken girl that I was completely falling head over heels in love with her. I was truly so enamoured with Mary that her curiosity was no big deal for me. But it was for the rest of the people in later stages.

One day I was off with her riding the horse and showing her the countryside and then we had a race. And I let her win. She was happy and overjoyed by her win that she hugged me so tight that day. I was a bit hesitant but then I hugged her back. She was like the soft comfortable little world welcoming me in her arms. And then she whispered something in my ears.

'I LOVE YOU TONY' my eyes were wide open in surprise. It was the damn thing I felt for her and I hugged her tightly right away to never let her go.

'I LOVE YOU MARY' - And we exchanged our rings as a happily married couple in the town. Everyone including Joseph was happy for our union. My parents were in tears but they were happy tears as Vivaians as you see. Our town partied late that night celebrating our happiness and spreading it among all. Joseph, Mary's family, and everyone were enjoying their life at the Viva City party.

So now everyone was back to their lives. And we two shifted in this house of ours in a few days. Everything was going great intact splendidly. We worked together, helping each other out and spending our time. Joseph used to visit our place quite often now and we all three used to have the best time of our lives. Our parents used to visit us too on weekends. We used to have our family weekend together. As some time passed, Mary wanted to start our own family. So I did want the same. We even had our parents suggesting the same all the time since we got married. We were asked by my mother to receive blessings from the town spirit too.

Till now Mary had only heard the name of it and she used to think it's the happiness that we had in our town which was named so by the folks. But as I took her to the woods to perform prayers and rituals out there, she was quiet for some time. She was confused and hesitant to perform any kind of such ritual. For her it was some kind of superstition that we town people were following, so she refused to do so though she still respected the woods and felt they were an essential part of our biosphere. City people, you know right, they have answers to everything and explanations and theories too. I was okay with her act but this made my mother worried a bit. She was now feeling guilty of her daughter in law insulting the Forest God. She even went on her own to apologise to the town spirit. Though she wasn't sure if, the woods had forgiven her or not. Days passed, and Mary started having problems with few of the things like us renting out our place to visitors for free though we didn't rent our new home since it had only one room and a hall. So she used to tell mother and father to rethink about it and change with time. This wasn't easy for the parents to understand and somehow I found them being upset about it. As a Vivaian we weren't supposed to be unhappy. I wanted to stop Mary from bothering our parents but then I couldn't do that even since this might hurt her.

Things in my life were slowly and slowly changing and hence, my parents' lives were affected. I wasn't able to realise at first and was okay with most of the changes but then when I saw my parents worry, I couldn't hold back. We had an argument between us, Mary, and me, for the very first time in our happy married life. She felt that it was all happening because my parents were not ready for new changes and to accept the practical world outside. Also she had a problem with our customs that we performed since she had started calling them superstitions and myths created by people who never saw the actual world. This made me sad to know her feelings about us all. Maybe she needed time to adapt and that made me okay to accept a few things for now.

This story was not just of one house but somehow my parents' house was also disturbed and slowly and slowly the issues spread like poisonous fumes around. Like a disease, it was catching people and they were changing in a way they weren't supposed to. After all, we were forgetting about the town spirit that we need to live up with. I wasn't really caring about it first nor were the people around as from where it initiated, the vibes, spreading all around and contaminating the air.

My wife was pregnant by now. It was her fifth month and she was keeping well. Although my mother still wanted her to at least apologise to the spirit God in her heart only to make things easy. But Mary wanted not to encourage such acts of misbelief. She continued her rebel and she was okay with it with zero regrets. But there was still one thing in Mary's head that was bothering her. She felt that since we were going to have our family, our baby we need to look after our expenses well. So she often asked me to ask my parents to rent out for cash so that we all could make it work for the whole family. We had enough fights on this topic and now things were getting worse day by day. She was having the reluctant behaviour of not hearing what we all believed and we were adamant not to change a single rule.

One day, as I came back from my parents' house, I saw Mary waiting for me. She seemed disturbed so I asked what had happened. To which she started yelling and talking all wrong about my ideology, my way of living. We had a huge argument and in the heat of the moment she cussed me and went back to the room and locked it from inside. I heard her crying for the first time and I got agitated now. I slammed the door behind me and went back to my parents place. Mary came out of the room after some time and found that I hadn't returned. She then went to the bathroom and there was a tap open. And she slipped. That was all for our happy world to end. She had a miscarriage and now she could never give birth to a child. I was furious about it like how could she do this to me. I left my place to stay with my parents for some time. Mary was now left in pain, heartbroken and in a deep feeling of GUILT. She was now not at all the same woman I knew. She was nervous, sad, and filled with remorse. And wherever she went she spread the same vibe. People in the town started having problems in their lives. They all were worried now. They went to the woods to offer prayers and conduct rituals. But all they could recall during the practice was all their pain and disappointments and misery in their lives. It felt as if the woods were reflecting their life back to them since they were coming in pain and offering pain to the spirit and it was returning them the same. Earlier people were happy, so they spread happiness around and received happiness as a blessing from the spirit but now they had all bad things to offer and so was their world turning dark and bad.

This was upsetting everyone in the town including my family too. They were now not having any kind of gathering to avoid that disease from spreading around. There was not a single happy face to be seen in the town now. Although I had my furies go away with time and I came back to my home again. But we were never like before now. Not so lively and supportive or even a bit happy or enjoying life. It wasn't the same anymore. We were just breathing and surviving and now the town and also stopped welcoming visitors. Some of them continued but now they charged money for that since they now felt they were losing life and they had less of whatever they deserved. The feeling of satisfaction was gone. People started turning greedy, jealous, unhappy, and dissatisfied. They were all in pain. Love was no longer their cure or medication.

People were crying in front of the woods to get better and it was actually worsening the situation. I saw my wife working the whole day like a dead soul with no joy in her eyes. I felt something was wrong, but not in her, instead something was wrong with me. I realised how lonely she must have felt the whole time losing her dream, her life and then me leaving her on her own. It was me who was wrong all the time and not her. And yes she was right that we need to change and I changed for her. I was supposed to be her life support and I was making it difficult for her. So, I stood up against all odds and decided to make her comfortable and relaxed. It took me a long time but it did work. We decided to start our family, so we adopted a little angel. She was seven years already and we gave her our world. It's then when I realised the magic or the blessings were not in the woods but it was all within us to make ourselves blessed and happy again.

But things were different for the town now. Their beliefs were so strong and powerful that the woods were actually answering their pain with pain, their fear with fear, their guilt with guilt and it was the living mirror now for the whole town. It was no longer what it was called as the Viva City. This made them mad at petty things. Soon people started seeing our family as the only happy family in the town. For they now felt that it was all because of Mary that the woods have cursed them and only if she apologise things might change back to what they were before. My parents too were on their side now. Although I tried hard to make them understand how wrong they had been interpreting the whole town spirit thing since ages and how they need to modify a few things to adapt with the changing time. But no one was interested in thinking about it for even a second.

The worst thing to happen was that they started cussing Mary for not being a town spirit supporter. They wanted her to leave the town if she wanted to go against their customs. I couldn't take this anymore and

I stood up against all of them but that worsened the case. They said that she was a witch and she had done some find of black magic on me. I wasn't ready to give up this early as she was my life. Also my little daughter shouldn't suffer therefore I sent her to her uncle Joseph for a few days till the situation was under control. I knew if Mary went out of the town she wouldn't have her way in and this would be of no use then.

Days passed but people grew more and more furious and they started throwing stones at our doors and windows to terrify us. Mary was frightened she had never seen those folks so mad and crazy filled with revenge. Few days later my mother passed away and I went to attend her funeral. I was sad now, although for Vivaians deaths were celebrating end of a happy time and starting of a new happy life. But now I was no more having the spirit of town. I cried at her funeral sitting alone after everyone was gone. My father came to me to say that everything would be alright but he himself knew nothing was right and things might never get right. He too had tears in his eyes and we both then walked home. Mary couldn't attend the last rites since I had asked her to stay back because of the fury people had against her. I sat with my father in his house for around 5 pm someone screamed -'there is a fire down the street,' father and I came outside to see where the fire was caught. I suddenly realised it was coming from the street I lived on. I ran down the street like a lightening energy filled in me. It was maybe the adrenaline rush. I wished it wasn't what my mind was asking me to think or worry about.

My father too followed me but he couldn't keep up with the pace. As I reached on the spot, everything was gone. EVERYTHING WAS GONE FOREVER! MY WORLD WAS DESTROYED IN SECONDS AND I COULD DO NOTHING ABOUT IT!

I fell on my knees, tears rolling down my eyes. My throat was choked from not being able to inhale air for a few minutes. My father kept his hand on my shoulder. We both had lost our love that day. We couldn't help each other but just be there for each other."

"Did she really die? Oh no, no this was not supposed to happen. I told you the people are insane here," cried the anxious me.

"It's not like they weren't always like this. It's just that they gave up their happiness over petty things in life," exclaimed the old man.

"I too had a family. And I can understand what it means to lose your loved one. They snatched your love and now they are snatching mine. We have to end this all at once," called out the rage and insecurity in me.

Tony was quiet and was looking at me in despair and all he wanted to vent out my heart and head too. I was so frustrated and restless that I started lamenting over how the world was not a happy place for me as I started up with the real story of my life. My roots, my everything that meant something to me somewhere, my sweet little world and the story of a boy who had it all from life and then finally wanted to see his life happy with his brother that he happened to meet at a stage when he had no one around. All I dreamt of was living life together and to the best we could. But every story has a nasty past as I already stated that the boy who happened to be me was all alone for so long before I came across Tim. It was about my initial childhood days. When I was a kid back then, I had a wonderful life with a happy family of four- my father, my mother, my little sister Susie, and me. It was more about my little sister- SUSIE.

(MY BACK STORY)

"Susie was a very decent kid with her aspirations soaring high in life." She believed in so many unreal things that often made it difficult for us to help her in differentiating between reality and thoughts. Also she was quite naïve to understand people and their stories. For her everything she heard had an existence. Her being of a very tender age, we were adamant to accept the facts of her fantasy world that had made home in her little heart. All we wanted was for her to live in a real practical world. Our parents had always adored her for being the younger child of home. She was seven years younger to me and I had been in love with her existence. Everything was so perfect in the beautiful world of ours. My father used to work in a Publication Department of one of the leading local dailies. He used to bring up articles and writing works at home too, working all his nights in framing visions of masses. And that's how I gained my interest in writing business. My mother being a housewife, working effortlessly all day to help us all, keeps us up with the pace of the world.

She was a perfect example of patience and compassion and not to forget the kindness that she bestowed on everything that moved with life in it.

She said that we must respect nature and it helps us live better. Also everyone around in our neighbourhood was quite fond of her. My mother was a divine woman with fewer expectations but more acceptances towards life and people. For her world was a happy place if we viewed it through her spectacles. Also when she was unmarried she had been a Social worker and because of that too she loved serving the universe. Her caring and loving nature had made us more mischievous at times and my father used to be worried about that. For he wanted us to behave in a certain manner which he called were basic ethics and etiquettes of our family. He believed in inculcating true morals at a very young age in order to frame a strong character of ours. So he was basically a strict father but filled with love and affection in his heart with no regrets. All he wanted his children to lead a successful life at later stages like every parent's dream. We were a small family but a happy and complete family.

But he didn't know what his children were up to. We never wanted to offend our parents but our dreams were more like a rebelling heat for our parents to accept. Also for me I grew to understand with time and change a few of my thoughts and likings but for my little sister her thoughts shaped in a very different way that became hard for them to understand or even digest. But still somehow we managed to let her life bloom with happiness and joy. As she was of a tender age, we thought that things might be okay for her when she will be of a certain age or at a specific stage of life. We had the happy days, the okay days, and sometimes not so good days but as a family we never threw each other alone in any situation.

But you know how life goes. It can never be a smooth journey. So was it with me too.

It was one day when SUSIE..." something interrupted us as I was narrating my heart out to Mr Tony.

CHAPTER

11

Busted!!!

As we were busy hearing about each other's stories, we didn't realise we spent hours in there. My heart was clenched in pain and fear to whatever I heard that day. Also I was reminded of my broken life and the long-time pain and guilt I was carrying with me since ages. Suddenly someone knocked at the door. And we both paused for a moment. It was my turn to narrate my part.

"Hurry, hide somewhere inside. You shouldn't be seen by anyone here. No worries, my granddaughter is at her school now. Don't worry, just hide," hushed Tony.

I tiptoed quietly and went inside the room to hide beneath the bed as it was the only place I couldn't be spotted at first glance or a normal search.

And then I heard voices outside in the hall.

"You, old crazy fellow, how dare you? Don't you get that you are ruining the town rules and going against the law," bashed a heavy furious voice aiming at Mr Tony.

"I didn't do a thing Sir. I am sorry I don't get what you are talking about?" as I heard a calm gentle voice of the old man.

"Don't fool me Tony. I know your story. You have been a great rebel and threat to our society. You should be thankful they didn't throw you away," groaned a second but familiar voice.

It seemed there were two people in the house. One obviously with a heavy voice was of the sheriff but I wasn't able to recall the second one.

"Enough of it, , I had it for a long time. You need to come with me to the police station. This is illegal what you are doing," ordered the sheriff.

"But what did I do wrong?" asked the confused old man in a whining tone.

I just heard their footsteps receding towards the main door and they were all gone. They took him with them and now I was damn scared what would happen next. I knew Mr Tony was not at all a criminal though, to be carried away like this. The criminals were the people of the town that were once innocent beings. I came out of the hiding place and ran to the window to see who the other person was.

It was someone who hated me the most in the town. Yeah, you got that right. It was the fruit vendor, maybe he was the one following me till here and telling about my whereabouts to that sheriff. I almost forgot to ask the most important thing from Mr Tony. The letter and the pen I got with me, I forget to enquire about the same. How stupid of me. Also I didn't know if he would be charged with something or released soon or not. All I could now remember were the scary truths that he told me about. What would be his fate now? I didn't even know what was waiting for me next.

I thought of following them in order to make sure if Mr Tony was treated right. I saw them at a distance; they were having some arguments while walking down the lane. All I wanted was for him to be safe as he was the actual spirit of this broken world. I was so tremendously terrified by the people around and their beliefs that I almost wanted myself to be an invisible guy at once. They were murderers and scavengers having no emotions, no heart, no kindness nor even love for the world.

The sheriff took Mr Tony to the station and the fruit man also accompanied him which was bothering me now. Since he was the most brutal of all, filled with so much aggression and hatred. I just went near the station to peep inside and see if he was safe or not.

"You are marvellous old flesh. I wish the woods had taken you before anyone. You deserve to die," busted the fruit vendor on Mr Tony.

"Hold on pal. I will not die till the world sees you all scavengers, muddle headed ruthless demons. I want the world to see how humans can go crazy for not accepting the changes and the world around them. I pity you all," laughed the old man.

"Hey, you moron, just shut up! You want to destroy us? You are breaking the town spirit since ages and that won't happen ever, again," while the sheriff shouting at him and hitting him hard.

What exposing thing were they talking about? Did you get that? Ahn, let me explain to you the story that we didn't complete. Let's just rewind back to the time at Mr Tony's house. And let's just rewind and go to the part where he said his wife was burnt down in her own house. Yeah there after you heard my story but Mr Tony had more to add on. And here it goes in his words -

'With time my wounds healed but the scars were left behind.' My little daughter stayed with her uncle for her schooling and I used to go to their place to visit her. She was growing up so fast and I wanted her to keep away from the world I came from. As a child, she was very sweet and kind hearted. She was not so mischievous like other kids. She loved her uncle and her parents too but she didn't know that her mother had died. I always used to tell her how much her mother missed her but she was ailing and couldn't meet her as she wanted to keep her safe. Though at times she really wanted to see her mother, Uncle Joseph used to keep her busy with games and all other stuff. As she grew younger and she was 22 now, she had completed her graduation from a great college in psychology degree in the city and wished to surprise her father that was me fortunately, with her arrival at the town - Viva City. Though she had never been to the town before, only the last time she was there was when she was 10 years old. She waited all these years to make a fresh start from her own hometown.

I never knew she wanted to be back. And then one day I saw her standing at my doorstep. I was so excited and emotional to see her. My eyes were filled with tears but

I was a bit worried too for her to see the world of darkness in here. She hugged me and that comfort she had in her arms made me burst out into tears. She was amazed to see how emotional I was but she thought it was all because she had returned after so long.

"Where is Ma? Let me surprise her as well," she said excitedly and rushed inside to check in the room while me standing at one place in trauma and pain. She came outside and her expressions were now a confused one.

"Where's mom? Did she go outside? Ah, I will have to wait for her to come," sighed Isabelle.

Oh I forgot to tell her beautiful name Isabelle that was chosen by her mother, Mary, when she first saw her in the orphanage. And now I was left with no answers and explanations to what she was going to witness or hear. I stood still at the same place with my face dropping down in agony. Isabelle saw the pain in my eyes and she understood immediately that something was wrong.

"What happened father? Tell me that everything is fine," in her anxious and scared voice.

I stood in silence not able to utter a single word. Her eyes filled with tears now rolling down her cheeks. She hugged me tight and cried a lot, so I did. But for the town, it wasn't over yet. They were still up with the notion that Mary had made all of us a rebel and our daughter might be the reflection of her.

Soon the news of Isabelle's arrival spread all around the town. People started worrying because of the young girl now. But to their surprise, Isabelle was very kind and soft spoken to even the rudest of them all. She had no grudges or hard feelings for anyone neither in the town nor even outside, do I believe. She was a great soul and a very humble lady. This charmed many young boys in the town. But she was reluctant to get married so soon. Although I wanted her to gel up with the town people to help her life get easy in here.

By her arrival almost everything was getting better in the town and also people saw her as no threat to their society so they were happy to accept her. She soon found her love in one of the military men living next to your landlord. They made a great match and I was okay with it so they got married eventually. She was living a happy life and she used to visit me often and she had already given up her profession by now but she didn't regret it. Her husband, James was a very eminent personality and had recently returned from the city like her. So they had found comfort in each other's world, understanding life, and accepting things.

Also he was a rich guy in ethics and wealth too. My world was somehow better than the old days but new people's arrival always brought insecurity in the hearts of the townies. Soon Isabelle gave birth to my beautiful granddaughter' Eva,' She was a very gentle and cute little angel. Within months they figured out a few weird things with the baby. Their baby was not normal like any other baby. They came to know that the child had developed autism with time they got to know what it exactly was. Isa was now worried about her child and used to spend *days crying at times and James couldn't help her out but they never abandoned their child. James was a supportive father until he was found dead in a mysterious manner at his own mansion. The whole town was in disbelief at what had happened. Some started calling out to Isa that she must have given birth to a witch that did take her husband's life. Some started calling Isa a witch. They weren't vocal to her on her face but Isa could know what gossip was going round the town.*

Isa kept a caretaker for her daughter so that she got the maximum attention. Although she never got away from her side, at times she thought of starting her business again. She thought of opening her psychology department in the town. But it was of no use. She understood with time that people in the town never wanted to change since they never had the acceptance of something going wrong in their lives. All they had a notion of theirs that the woods were to be worshipped and the glory of the town will be maintained likewise.

She even came to me to tell how the world in here was having strange disbeliefs and I was already aware about the same. I then told her the story of her mother, to which she cried and was left in shock to see how people here were not just superstitious but they were mentally not sound as well. She now decided to change the town for its good sake but I told her that was impossible to happen. Her mother tried the same but lost herself in the process. I was now worried for my daughter but she was reluctant to change her decision at any cost now. Also I knew my town people too that they won't change at all ever not in this birth.

Isa now used to visit the town less. She had the caretaker working for her with every outdoor chore. Instead she would plan up things to make a community free of the mental illnesses they were going through. Also at times she left Eva with me and I liked taking care of her. Isa often visited the woods to experience what everyone else believed. She was already worried about her only daughter and thought the town people might harm her in her absence.

While I wanted her to stay away from those woods since it would only bring misery to her life and Eva's life was also connected to hers now. So she needed to be more careful with whatever she did. She was quite disturbed by Mary's tragedy and couldn't sleep for nights. At first she thought of taking the new generation into influence since their beliefs were still under construction.

She started teaching in the local school although she was barely allowed at first. Thereafter she started introducing moral science topics in the class to involve children to follow good deeds and ethics since the town was now lacking it the most. Slowly and slowly she started telling students how some beliefs or things we see are not the same as we assume and started including the example of the town spirit. She taught them how to find happiness in themselves rather than materialistic things. Children started following her and in a few days she managed to influence a few minds to change for better. Also she had asked her students to promise that they won't be letting this secret out- the real secret of happiness or else they would lose it and they will never ever be happy. Young minds started believing what they were being taught. Also not even a single child told anyone else about that. They loved their teacher and they trusted her. But soon their ideology and her teachings were being reflected in their behaviour too. Some parents were okay with it while some became suspicious and got worried. They became curious to know who was really teaching them this all. So they convinced their children to be true to them. And a few of them told their parents about Isa. And this was the end of her teaching.

Isa was now sad and she started hating the very sight of the town people. Also she had to take care of her daughter as well. Things were not how she wanted in her world. But soon the town people started with their dirty games to keep her shut with her opinions. It was the time when they were up with the new rule of everyone offering prayers to the town spirit in the woods. But now they have changed it into a terrible heart wrenching law. It was the most brutal of all. They now thought of eliminating the negative souls from the town by offering them to the woods. It wasn't all they planned to make Isabelle suffer so that she surrenders to the town spirit or else they would punish her same.'

I was just into the thoughts of how mean they all had turned when suddenly while eavesdropping at the station, I accidentally happened to touch something very cold while trying to hide beneath the window peeping inside. I looked around to see a pale body of a girl standing next to me with that scary face. I lost my balance and fell down since I got scared. The sound of falling was audible inside the station even and the three freaked out to hear the sudden sound.

"Who's that? Who's outside? I am going to get you fella," called out the sheriff in an anxious voice.

I got up to run and save my life since I knew if I got caught things might not be good for me at all. I just heard them shouting behind me chasing me for a while. I was safe by now as I had reached my premises. I knew they hadn't seen me clearly and now I could stay at my place and rest for the day.

CHAPTER

12

The Revenge Game

It was midnight and I was in my deep sleep by now. I heard someone calling out my name from a distance. The voice was too familiar and so heart-warming. And then I saw Tim at a distance. Laughing out loud and calling me to join him. He seemed to be standing on a beach and then he started walking towards the sea. While I saw him slowly and slowly going further. I asked him to stop since it was very dangerous and it could be fatal as well. But he wasn't listening, just happily moving forward and then I ran to just drag him back but till then he was completely gone.

And I woke up terrified from a bad dream. But I could still hear someone calling out my name. It was coming from down stairs. I was a bit nervous but I needed to check who it was. I took out the torch from the side table. And slowly walked towards the door and then I looked in the other rooms as well but the voice seemed to have been coming from downstairs so I just threw the light on the stairs to go down. And then as I reached, I checked every room down there as well but there was no one. I sighed in relief and was just moving back and as soon as I turned by I was frightened to see Mr Tony standing right behind me. At first I got scared and almost jumped in fear but then was relaxed to see it was him and not any ghost or spirit.

He held my wrist and said-

"Hurry out now! They are going to kill you. Come with me," pulling my arm while rushing towards the main door.

I was scared to even ask a question and followed him while he pulled my arm all along the way. I wanted to ask what he was doing this late at my place. And how did he even get out of the prison. But he was in such a hurry that I couldn't even figure out what was exactly happening. He rushed to the woods and pulled me too while I was walking in difficulty as the grass was too tall to walk through.

"Why are we heading to these deadly woods? Won't they find us here?" I asked him in an innocent voice and in worry.

"Just hurry! They will tear you apart! Follow me," said Mr Tony hastily, still not ready to stop at any cost.

Suddenly I fell on my knees as there was a big rock in the middle of the way. And it hurt me badly while my hand slipped off his grip. It was bleeding and it was paining a lot.

"Can't we just hide instead of just running aimlessly?" as I raised my head up to ask my partner to slow down a bit.

But to my utter surprise, there was no one there., I wasn't able to see Mr Tony anywhere nor even at a distance. All I could see were the trees surrounding me and it seemed I was in the middle of the woods exactly at the centre. Where did he go? Just in a flash of seconds! I was worried and horrified at the same moment not knowing what to do. I looked around and it seemed the whole place was revolving around me and I felt catastrophic at the moment and fainted.

As I woke up with a jerk, I found that it was just a dream. I sighed in relief and was about to go back to sleep when I heard a voice again coming from downstairs and that was the same voice I heard in my dream. This time I thought of being careful and didn't wish to check who it was but my mind was asking me to look for it. So I got up with my torch and went directly downstairs to check. There was still no one there and when suddenly I turned around, it was him. He grabbed my hand and asked me to leave the house to save myself.

I tried not to go with him but it felt like some energy was controlling me and I couldn't release myself from his grip.

"No, not that way. I saw this all," I yelled at the old man.

"Oh come on, what are you talking about? Just keep moving. You don't know how dangerous they are," said the old man in a concerned tone.

I followed him and again we were heading to the woods.

"I said just leave me. Who are you?" I forcefully got out of his hands.

"I am your friend. You forgot? I am the only person who can help you, just come with me," he slowly grabbed my wrist again.

It was a terribly cold touch and I put my eyes on his hands only to find out that they were pale like a dead corpse. I was terrified and I looked at his face but his whole face was covered in scars. I cried out loud in fear. And then I almost managed to get off from his hold. As I ran back towards the house, I saw that the woods were getting even deeper. There was no end to it. It seemed I was just running deep into it rather than getting out of it. I kept running, not looking behind at all, scared and sweating like hell. And then suddenly I stopped, there was a man standing at a distance, I turned around to change my path and then somebody clenched my throat with his bare cold hands. His grip was so tight that I wasn't able to breathe at all. I tried removing his hands but couldn't. And then I choked and suddenly everything started to fade off in front of my eyes. Slowly my eyes closed.

After a while, I heard someone calling out my name. I tried opening my eyes, it was dark and I was in a room. That was my room. I was on my bed. I then heard voices again but this time they were too many. I was shivering now in fear as I got up and sat on my bed. The voices were coming from outside my house but from a distance. I got to look through my window at what exactly was happening. I saw a group of people dragging someone, struggling hard to get released, towards the deadly woods. I was too scared to even stop them or even check out what was going on. So I was just peeping through the window and trembling in fear to witness the incident. I then saw them throw his body into the woods while some were returning back. And then I saw something unusual, the little ghost girl at a distance staring at me. My eyes got stuck at her and then I shook my head a bit to regain my senses. To which I saw that a fat guy was standing at the same place looking at my house. He was in uniform - The sheriff.

I immediately hid myself and then a few moments later peeped back through the window to see if they were still there or not. But they were all gone. I was worried about what had happened and this made me believe that maybe something worse had happened with my brother too. Maybe there was no chance of getting him back. I was kind of losing hope and now I didn't even have faith in God to make things right anymore. All I wished for was just a nightmare like the previous ones. I tried sleeping but it was becoming quite a hard task for me now.

I closed my eyes to make it easy for me to sleep soon. And it did work. I was now sleeping in my bed when in the middle of the night someone just knocked at the main door. It was quite loud and clear due to the pin drop silence at that time. I was now scared to even go down stairs. I checked my watch to see it was 4 am in the morning now. I gathered some courage and went downstairs to see who it was.

And again as I opened the door there wasn't anyone present. I was about to close the door immediately when a hand stopped it from closing. My eyes popped out in fear again. My forehead was full of sweat. But it seemed like a human hand.

"Help me please! Please help me!" as the young-middle aged woman cried with tears rolling down her cheeks.

She seemed fine other than traumatised and didn't feel suspicious or something. I opened the door a bit further, not fully opening it.

"What do you want? Who are you?" as I asked her in a terrified fumbling voice.

"Please let me in, they killed my husband. They will kill me too. Please just let me in. Please help me!" the woman cried while sobbing badly and loudly.

At first I felt like closing the door but the woman seemed genuine and the scene felt more like a reality than a dream. My heart was still pounding rapidly and I could even suffer from a nervous breakdown but I somehow gathered courage and gulped in the saliva almost choking my throat. I took a deep breath and then opened the door wide. At first I had a glance at her completely to find if anything was wrong with her. She seemed all okay. So I let her close the door behind me. It was dark inside the house due to no electricity. But I have kept a few candles to deal with it. I lit up the living area and asked her to sit and offered her some water to which she refused.

She was a well-built woman and was an epitome of beauty as I could still see it through the dim light of the candles and the lamp. She was shivering in fear and cold. So I made coffee for her to help her get warmed up. Also I lit up the fireplace that I haven't used since we first arrived here. At first it served as the showpiece for the house but now it was immensely used to brightening the room at night.

"Are you fine now, ma'am? Please don't be terrified you are safe inside. I mean at least from the town people," while recalling my tragic experiences.

"Thank you so much for letting me in. These people are not humans. They are animals. They killed my husband and now they want to kill me and my daughter too," as the woman started wiping again.

"Hey, no, no please don't cry. You need to be courageous. We will figure out something, don't worry," as I tried to console her.

It was turning bright outside. It was almost morning now. I myself was worried to have a stranger come up with a problem for me when I was already having one foot in the coffin. But now we had to be out of here by anyhow since it was no longer a place to live or even survive. She was right, they were hunting like wolves moving in packs and ending up lives at midnights. My only wish to see Tim was now almost finished since there was no chance of me surviving here. Also Mr Tony was arrested and I wasn't sure what was waiting for both of us next. And now this woman, who had appeared in the middle of nowhere and was crying for help was making me worry for my life too. Why on Earth did they not understand the pain of others? Why wasn't it the same Viva City that was supposed to be once? Why was this place no more for humans? Their beliefs were killing their own happiness and they were hardly realising it. Even if someone realised they didn't let him live any longer. AND WHY WAS THIS PLACE A LIVING HELL? JUST WHY?

The stranger at my house was more like keeping a time bomb at my place since I knew people were chasing her and they might get to know her whereabouts soon. Although my luck had saved me for the last time, I didn't want to end my life here because of being a helping hand to someone I had never met before. But I couldn't even be mean to someone all because I wanted to save myself which was totally a selfish act of mine. It was already morning by now and I needed to ask her the necessary questions to know if she was really a victim and not someone from the other side hiding up her real intentions just to set me up for the last ritual. Also I was afraid that if she turned innocent she might take me the other way instead but I needed to take chances for my own sake now.

She was sitting in the living area quietly but now much more relieved than before. I just went up to her to start up a conversation on my own.

"So, how are you doing now? Is there anything I can bring for you?" I asked the lady in a very hesitant humble voice.

"I am much better. Thank you. I am fine as of now. You can please continue with your business. I will just leave for the city in a while. Sorry for troubling you so much," said the lady in distraught. I could still see fear and pain in her eyes. So I didn't say a word. Maybe it was not the right time.

I then prepared breakfast for the two of us. But she didn't eat; she said she was not having an appetite though I insisted she have a little bit but she refused. I ate my breakfast and then cleaned up the kitchen and utensils. I made a coffee for her and then sat down on a nearby chair.

"Well, can I ask you something if you don't mind?" as I was still dubious about enquiring.

"Yeah, sure, you can go ahead," said the lady in a timid voice.

"Where do you live by the way? I mean I haven't seen you in the town though I don't know much of them but still, just asking," while controlling my nervousness.

"I just stay nearby…"

Suddenly a SMASH was heard and we both were startled by the noise. I turned back to find out that somebody had thrown a stone at the kitchen window that I had repaired a day before.

"Oh, God! Not again. What a nitwit they are. I hate them to the core," agitated me in an annoyed tone.

I went to look outside if there was somebody or some kids like the other days. But there was no one.

I was about to return back but then I saw someone coming from a distance. It was the sheriff. I was frightened and I turned back to tell the lady to hide somewhere upstairs. She tiptoed and went upstairs and I cleaned up the place a bit to make it look as if I was the only one in the house. But I was worried about why that guy had turned up at my place. Was he in a mood to arrest me or just kill me? I got nervous as the door was thudded by the big guy. My eyes were wide open and I got confused, unable to decide what to do next.

He started banging the door with more force and calling out my name. I was scared to open it but I had to or else he might not spare me at any cost. So I went with my shaky legs towards the door to open and meet my fate.

As I opened the door, the sheriff was staring right back at me with his eyes filled with rage. I started sweating by now. But then I had to not give up on my God. To my surprise the sheriff's face expression changed to a smiling one. At first I got so puzzled to see what just happened but then he started talking nicely with me. I didn't utter a word as I was not able to get anything whatever he said.

"Cool down Mr Writer, why are you so stressed? I was here for the case you had filed a week ago. I hope you remember that," laughed the sheriff.

"Yeah, of course it's about my missing brother. But...," I was still confused by the behaviour of the big guy.

"But, what Sir, why do you seem to be so confused? Don't you wish to see your brother again? I am here to help you. Won't you let me in?" the sheriff asked with a smiling face.

"Ah nothing's like that. Yeah please come in," as I tried staying normal in my senses.

I was scared for a moment and hesitant too but I didn't want him to get suspicious. What if he was here to find the missing lady? And what if he finds her in here? My life could be ruined any moment now. So I decided to play careful with the man. But he was not at all interested in finding my brother so why is he interested all of a sudden?

"Do you want to ask something Sir?" As the sheriff sat down on the couch and was looking at my pale face.

I was out of my thought chain as soon as I heard his question. My throat was becoming dry in fear now.

"Hmm? Oh, no, no Sir. I just wanted to see my brother again. Do you have any way to get to him?" I tried being anxious and worried though as I was in real life for my brother but at the moment my facial expressions weren't in place.

"Yeah, so where did you see him last?" inquired the sheriff in a serious tone.

"It was the woods as I told you last time too. I didn't find him thereafter. I even searched the woods on my own but all I could find there was some...," as I paused all of a sudden since I was about to say something wrong while going with the flow. I just had a glance at the sheriff's face who was expecting for something unusual to hear but I managed to save myself for the moment.

"I mean it was just woods around and it was too dark in there to even see anything properly. But I am sure he wasn't there. I had searched every corner of it," as I drowned in guilt.

"Umm, okay so you say you didn't find anything there. Okay. But what were you two doing there before this all happened?" the curious sheriff asked while giving a firm stare.

I didn't want to let him know what I saw that day so I just changed the scenario.

"We both were just walking around randomly, having our talks. And then he fell on the ground and thereafter he went missing," as the pain of losing him was eating me from inside as I recalled the incident in my head.

"But you were saying something else that day. Umm I see. So I heard someone saying you weren't putting up with him very often. You must have had issues among yourselves," while the sheriff tried to trap me into something unknown.

"No Sir, it wasn't that way. He is my brother. Why would I even do that?" I spoke up for myself as I got a bit hyper to hear such allegations.

"I heard that you had a squabble that day too. Mr Writer," while smirking, "why do I feel it was you who wanted to get rid of him. You were so entitled to be the master that you couldn't bear him raising his voice in front of you!"

"Why would I do that to my brother? What nonsense are you talking about?" As I got furious to hear such pathetic blames out at me.

"Well that's because you are a lunatic. You are the devil! You get that! YOU ARE THE DEVIL!!! JUST LEAVE THIS PLACE!!!" yelled the sheriff while leaving the house and threatening me of the consequences of the same.

I was stunned for a while. This was so disgusting to even think of. The sheriff was having the audacity to make fun of what they did to my brother. He was here just to trigger me and just to scare me off from here. How stupid I was to just believe him once again. This town was now going way too far and this was making me crazy now.

But for the moment I was relaxed that it wasn't the lady he came for. So I just went outside to make sure he really left the place. And then I closed the door behind and went upstairs to ask the lady to come out as she was out of danger now. It was quite strange that she wasn't there. I looked every room upstairs and every possible place to see if she was hiding but no, there was no one. How was this possible? I called out for her again to make sure if I was messing up with my brain again. But to my surprise, there was pin drop silence. I even checked the rooms downstairs too. There was no sign of her.

Did she jump through the window? But how would that be even possible? The windows were locked from inside and it was impossible for her to go through the closed window. But where did she go and how did she even disappear like this? I am getting mad now. I really was feeling like a lunatic. Was there another ghost in here? No but she wasn't there before.

My head started aching now with all the questions and unusual things happening around. But who was she? I felt like I was attracting the deadly spirits in my house. It could be because of the woods you see, there had already been so many murders in this town. But she seemed so fine, no difference in human flesh. Whatever she was or whoever she was, I needed to get it all right.

I made tea for myself and sat at my writing desk. I once used to spend my whole day there but now I wasn't longing for anything other than surviving in this nasty cruel world. All I could do now was to get Mr Tony to help me and then I needed to flee from this place as soon as possible.

But how was I supposed to free him from there? That sheriff could almost shoot me if he ever sees me again. Also it was very difficult to avoid that fruit vendor too. He was a total creep in real life. But I had to do something or else my doomsday would be any sooner.

I made a decision now. If I get out of this town now, I won't leave my brother and that old man behind. So I wore a hoodie and then went down the street covering my face with a scarf wrapped around. People were so busy with their own lives that they weren't really bothered by me passing by. As I was passing by Mr Tony's place, I suddenly remembered about his granddaughter. Who had she been with last night then? I stopped as I got worried. I went towards his door and it was locked. Where was the child but? The other day she was supposed to be at school.

"But she can't stay in school the whole day. Then where did she go?" As I started talking to my own self while getting worried more and more.

"What if I check her school? But where is her school? Oh God I can't even take anyone's help," as I was so tense that I started biting my nails in worry.

I was feeling sorry for the little girl who suffered so much because of the ugly rituals and beliefs of the Vivaians, the so -called happy citizens of the town. But all I could do now was to just get the old man out of the custody of that scatter brained sheriff.

Rescue Tony

I headed towards the station now. At first I tried to look for the mad fruit vendor, but to my relief his stall wasn't there yet. So I walked up straight to the station. I had no clear plan what to do next but was ready to face any consequences if I got caught. I looked through the window only to find the missing sheriff. Maybe he was somewhere outside or could be in the restroom as well. But I had to take a chance anyhow. So I looked around to make my first move and then crept in quietly while being extremely careful and alert. I saw Mr Tony lying curled up on the ground in a small cell that was apparently the only temporary cell available there. His eyes were closed and it seemed that he was in a deep sleep. I could see him shivering a bit in between as it was quite cold in there. I went up quickly to the desk of the sheriff and looked for the keys in the drawers.

Alas there wasn't any key in there. I looked in the cabinet nearby too but still couldn't find anything there. And then I heard footsteps and I was so scared for my life now.

"You? What are you doing here?" I turned back while my face turned red. But to my surprise it wasn't the sheriff but Mr Tony who was awake now from his sleep.

"Just go from here or else you will be punished like me," said the old man in a worried tone.

"No, I won't go without you. We will leave this place together," called out the rebel adamant inner me.

"Just tell me where the keys are, so that we make it real quick," as I asked the old man in a tensed voice.

He asked me to check the sling hung on the chair. Oh how foolish of me ignoring it the whole time. I hurriedly checked it properly to get the keys out and yes they were there. I then opened his gate to get him out and then we ran for our lives. We knew we couldn't go to our places anymore since they would definitely search there for us. So we decided to hide somewhere they would never think of. I secretly abandoned the town and Mr Tony guided me the way. And then as we were escaping I saw him taking the route to the woods. I stopped as I got a bit confused and blank at the moment.

"Why are we heading to those woods? That's the God damn place they would definitely find us and bury us as well," as I curiously threw a question at Mr Tony who was still moving.

He turned back and saw me standing at a distance with an expression of being sceptical about his lead. He came closer to me and put his hand over my shoulder to ease me out.

"Sir, You helped me right there. Let me help you here. You need to trust me. It won't harm you," as he gave a look of being confident about his move.

And then we two walked up to the woods, me quietly following his footsteps. I was kind of afraid of those woods at the current stage so I stuck closer to the old man leading the path. They were still dark with a narrow beam of sunlight penetrating through the canopy of the tall trees. The foliage of the trees was making it quite dense to look at, covering almost the whole sky above our heads. We were just walking and walking with my mind filled with fear and questions and lots of ifs and buts as well. And suddenly a concern arose in my head and I immediately stopped Mr Tony walking ahead.

"Mr Tony we left your Eva in there. Hurry we must get her out of there or else they won't let her live," as I was anxiously moving here and there not knowing exactly what to do next.

The old man was now quiet, standing in silence and his expressions were more like a heart broken person. I knew things were not so great in his life but he wasn't a timid guy to give up on life so easily. I was confused to see him not reacting to the situation and not keeping it quick for it was his granddaughter we were talking about at the moment.

"What's the matter? Why are you thinking so much? We can't leave her behind," as I emphasised asking him to go back.

"There's no use," said the old man in a low voice.

"What do you mean? How can you do this to your Eva? That's your only love left behind right?" In a concerned and agitated voice filled with emotions.

"Let's keep moving," as the old man sighed and started walking again.

"What? I won't. I am going back if you are not. I am not like you, you are such a cowardly man," I answered in a furious tone.

I was heading back to the town when I heard him yell from behind.

"YOU WON'T FIND HER!"

"At least I will try, not like you giving up without even trying once. I know what it feels to leave your heart behind," as I replied back in a loud tone while still moving.

"SHE IS GONE!" the old man yelled with his throat filled with emotions.

I stopped. What did he just say? That can't be true. He loved and protected her so well all these years and now things changed. Was it me who did that to them?

"She is gone. I lied to you that she was at school. She is gone and maybe she is with my Isa now, my daughter," the old man in a low emotional voice.

I wasn't able to speak a word further. I stood there for a long time recalling what all I did to bring trouble to their family. I felt sorry for all that happened to them. I turned back and ran towards him while hugging him tightly. He was quiet and it took him a few seconds to react to that. And then off we went.

It was afternoon by now. We were still finding a place to rest for the day. I was quite scared of the place because of all that had happened to me since I found that letter, which was now no longer the real concern. Also I hadn't shared anything about my experiences with those woods to Mr Tony yet. Anyhow he just knew about my brother going missing here. I was worried if we ever got caught, we might face a gruesome death but it was better to try than to give up so soon. Mr Tony was a kind man to hang on to but for the town he had now committed a crime that was not to be appreciated by anyone.

After a long walk we found a rock shelter among a few rocks in the middle of the jungle and we thought of staying there for the night. I was too tired by now and so was Mr Tony, so we sat down for a while. We were silent for so long and I wanted to talk to him but the guilt inside me was stopping me from doing so.

"I am sorry..." we both broke the silence at the same time as we looked at each other.

"No, I am sorry. I am really sorry. I have put you in deep trouble for no reason. My life was already messed up and now I have messed up your life as well," as I felt bad for Mr Tony for undergoing such injustice because of me.

"It's not your fault. I could have let you know sooner about what this place was so that you would have left early. Though I tried a bit to let you know by giving you signs instead of talking in person," confessed Mr Tony.

"What signs are you talking about? I didn't get you," me looking at his face with curiosity and doubt now.

The old man was looking at the ground now with a feeling of guilt he was carrying in there with him for all those months.

And then he spoke-

"The letter you received that day…"

"Oh, the letter was from you? So that was you all the time," as I was startled by the claim.

"Why didn't you let me know? That letter almost ruined my life for no reason. That letter acted like a bad omen for me the whole time. This could have been prevented only if…," as I cried in pain and complained.

"Only if I would have let you know it the very same day. I know I was wrong but all I wanted was to safeguard you and your brother," said Mr Tony in a low voice.

"I knew you might get alert by it but I wasn't aware that it might lead to something else as well. I thought threatening you and warning you might help you in a way getting away from this place. Also I didn't want to tell everything in the starting itself as I thought you might not take it seriously. Also I tried my very best to keep you safe from all those butchers at first. They all wanted to shove you off since the day you arrived but I tried convincing them that you might not harm them since you were a pure hearted person. I had already seen Tim coming up for groceries in the town and he was very generous and kind to everyone. They actually found him sweet and humble so they changed their thoughts about you as well. For them, their happiness was and is the most important thing and they thought you two were content in your lives full of happiness and prosperity and that might help the woods to spread the same in the town as well."

"But then why did you do that when everything was fine and okay with them all? What made you spoil it?" I cried in agony.

"But you weren't content," answered the old man.

"How can you even know that? Why did you even assume that on your own?" Me getting agitated and furious over the fact that it wasn't me who ruined it all but someone's assumptions landed us in this situation.

"I came to know it the day you started seeing the clothes hanging on to the rope next door. And it wasn't you alone who saw that, it was Tim too, your brother," said the old man.

"But how did you know that? I mean I never shared it with anyone. Does anyone live over there?" My head filled up with confusion and anxiety at the same time.

"It was Tim." He loved you the most and he adored you like his God. He had no one to look up to but only you he would cling to whenever he was in trouble or sad. He often came to my stall for vegetables and I used to talk to him a lot. He was a great kid with that soft heart of being tremendously honest and naïve. He never had any hatred for anyone in his life. Though, he claimed that he actually had a miserable one before meeting you. But he was happy to see you now and be with you now and forever. All he wanted was to stay with you happily. He used to tell me how you used to narrate stories for him every day. He almost told everything that happened with him all day long and eventually we became friends. I adored him too as my own grandson. But then one day he asked me about the house next to yours. And he told how he and you always saw the clothes hanging out there but you had never seen your neighbours in person. I got worried as you were now getting visions of something that was long gone. This made me think of all the miserable things that could happen to you and your little family. Though I never told Tim about the house since he was just a kid to understand and that might have impacted his little heart too.

I didn't want to scare him with the real facts about that place. So I thought of writing to you but wasn't sure what to write. I just wanted you to stay away from those woods because they were giving you visions then and now about the insecurities you owned. Yes it's true they do let you know your inner side. But it often becomes a curse for people since they are not so happy inside. So were you, you had something inside you that started haunting you in real life. It was never the letter but the suppressed misery in your heart that started scaring you. I don't know what it was and you know better what it is exactly about. The day you got the letter, I was sure of one thing that you might search for the address as well so I turned it in a way that it was coming from your neighbour's house. So that you think they are real people in there and that would have never made you anxious about their existence. But I was stupid enough to not think that you could even go and enquire in there. Though it was kind of part of my plan, Ben had come to the picture only to help me out with my plan. But as his father passed away due to sudden illness he gave up the job and went to the city to switch on to another life since life here was hard for people in pain and he knew that. Thereafter I was left alone to work on something I wanted. After that I don't know what exactly happened to you and why Tim went missing. Since I saw him last in the post office, I thought he was there to receive some kind of post. I knew he didn't know about the letter that time since he used to share everything with me whenever he met me," narrated the old man while feeling sorry for all that took place.

I was astounded to hear what he said. This was so new to me, and all this time I had been running after the wrong thing. It made me feel that all the miseries and mishaps were the result of my mental condition and hidden sorrows. Still, I had a few questions that were making their way out of my mouth now.

"And how did the town know that we were having visions? Why did they turn on us?"

"It was the query you made at the post office that day about that letter." I was afraid that you might find out about it, but the warning written on it puzzled the postmaster. He became concerned about you receiving a letter from someone unknown in the town about the woods. So, they held a meeting in the town to discuss your letter. I was also there. They asked every town person to find out who was responsible, but somehow they couldn't determine that. The sheriff led the meeting, following his grandfather's legacy, as he had once been the leader of the clan in his early days. He was welcomed by all the townspeople as their leader and always ensured that the town remained secretive, shielding the outer world from our affairs. However, I was fearful of getting caught too, so I decided to destroy any evidence that might lead them to me one day. Unfortunately, they eventually discovered my involvement. But before that happened, I gave the pen I used to write the letter to the sheriff himself on his birthday, viewing it as an opportunity to rid myself of guilt and fear of being caught. He appreciated and loved the gift, so I was relieved of the main evidence. Additionally, the witness of the case had already left town and was unwilling to return, so I was almost free of worry. Until then, nobody knew that you were experiencing any visions or anything of that sort. However, they were afraid of the disruption caused by the letter. They feared you might raise suspicions and uncover the hidden truth of Viva City, which made them anxious and hostile whenever they saw you. They started hating you without reason, believing that every misery in their homes was due to your attempts to expose their hidden secret.

By then, I was certain your curiosity would drive you mad, and you would seek answers and assistance. So, I aimed to create a distinction among all the people you had encountered so far. I was kind to you, which earned your trust and desire to connect. Initially, I was hesitant to help you, but by then, I knew it was almost over for both of us, as you had gone to report your missing brother at the sheriff's office. News of this spread like wildfire in town, causing everyone to fear the consequences. However, I don't know what happened to your brother exactly or who was responsible, as your brother was never a genuine threat to the people here. When we all gathered one night for a general meeting after your complaint, they all denied having harmed Tim. The sheriff too was now concerned, as this was the first missing person case, but sadly, it was not the last, as more townspeople reported their children missing thereafter. Perhaps you were unaware of this news, having been cut off from the town."

No one knows what actually was happening all at this corner. People were feeling scared of the woods now as you too were. But according to the clan's belief we are not supposed to shy away from our duties that we are supposed to offer to the giver of our life- the town spirit. So the sheriff decided to make you run away from the town. Therefore they regulate your electricity and the water supply so that it becomes hard for you to survive here. They started being rude to you all the time because of the hatred they carried for you.

After some days of spying on you, they found you meeting me in the town so I came under their radar. The sheriff knew my story of Mary and my daughter Isa and he thought that I was a threat for all since I might be taking revenge on my family by helping you out so they took me to the station. By now I was certain that he might kill me in no time and that's why I just wanted to see you safe and sound out of this town," claimed the old man.

"And what about Eva then, where is she? What happened to her?" I was in a state of anguish.

"She was with me till the day you first visited her. But, the very next day, when I was preparing food for her in the kitchen, I heard her last cry. And as I went inside to confront her, she wasn't there. I looked for her everywhere in the town and I couldn't find her. It was then some people disclosed a few incidents of their child going missing at home. I was broken and now I had nothing left to live for. It was Eva that was keeping me alive for so many years. I lost my wife, my daughter, and my granddaughter to this town," as he started weeping in pain.

"And how did Isa die…?"

"Isa was seen as threat to society when she started rebelling with the people ideology in here." Her caretaker was a boy from the town itself. He was not happy for all Isa planned to destroy the beliefs of his people. So he started putting sedatives in her tea every day to make her feel that she was having some kind of medical problem. And this might help him distract her from the issues she had with the people in the town. And one day she was on sedative when she fell off from the stairs and broke her lower femur bone. She was in a wheelchair after that and I took Eva to my place to take care of her but Isa stayed with us for a few days and then went back to her house since she didn't want to keep it shut for all. She used to have her caretaker at her place keeping the house tidy and taking care of her wants. She never knew who was behind her condition till then. She treated the caretaker as her own son. But she often hated visitors from the town since they used to come up to her place to just bash her with ugly words and to laugh on her condition. They all called her witch and said that she deserved what was going through as she had spoilt their kids and now they had turned into rebels. Therefore she started becoming ill and started losing mental health. She used to yell at people who turned at her place by saying that nobody lived in there and asked them to run away. The caretaker again started giving her sedatives to make her calm this time. Her condition was getting worse with time. But one day Isa saw her caretaker pouring something into her tea. She caught him and threatened to punish him as she thought he was after the wealth she owned at her precious house. And this scared the boy. So instead of revealing his real motive he hit her on her head with a china dish pot nearby and Isa fainted. He then strangled her with a black cloth till death. He knew nobody cared about her much and nobody would ever come to know till anyone comes up there. So he hid the body beneath the staircase and locked the house. I was worried about Isa and went to meet her one day but I saw the lock at the door so I went to see the caretaker instead. He said that she was out of town for her medical check-up and that somebody from the city had come to see her and he took her along with him. At first I thought it must be Joseph, her uncle and then I called him up to confirm. He didn't receive my call and I thought he might be busy. Isa was not picking my call too. I then got Joseph's call the other day. He asked me about my health and how Eva was doing. He then asked me about Isa if she was fine as he had called her some day and she had yelled at him on the phone while asking him not to call again and saying that nobody lived there. I was numb for a moment as Isa was supposed to be with him. I asked him if he was just playing some kind of dirty joke or prank. He denied in a serious note. We then realised that something was wrong at the moment. I went back to the caretaker to ask about what he was hiding. But till then he had committed suicide. I went back to Isa's place and by then Joseph had also arrived. We looked for her everywhere but couldn't find her. It was after a few months later that her body was recovered with the help of the police dog that the sheriff owned, from beneath the staircase, all rotten up and the whole place having a terrible stench in the whole house. I was broken apart and Joseph too couldn't bear the pain. We both were left in remorse and regret of letting her live in the town. Joseph asked me to go with him but I refused to leave my hometown where I had my most beautiful memories with my beloved ones. So I stayed back with my only granddaughter and the only reason left to live. The town was relieved to have got rid of my daughter. I knew how happy they were with my loss like always. They thought this might retain their peace but it wasn't so, their insecurities always got triggered with the slightest change that took place in the town. But by now I had understood and learnt how to keep distance from all their grievances and beliefs.

You know what they all never wanted to change and that's what made the real changes in their lives, the worst scenarios that hit their life. I never could have spared them for how they behaved with my loved ones when they were alive but I never wanted to stoop down to their level. I forgave them for all their foolish deeds and beliefs, as it was more like wrestling with a pig; you both get dirty and the pig enjoys it. With time they forgot all the pain and miseries for the moment as they were all self-created but for them it was Isa and now she was gone. So they shredded off their bag of misery and sorrows they carried for so long. And then one fine day you came to the town and became the talk of the town. The rest of the story is known to you now already," finished Mr Tony with a deep guilty tone.

I was left in trauma for a while and I kept quiet to analyse all that he narrated till now.

We both were in pain and filled with guilt by now. The long silence took over and we sat there for hours.

It was getting dark and we were least bothered about it at the moment. I now knew what made the fruit vendor mad and the reason for all those people to hate me so much. But at this moment I hated myself for not shedding off the baggage of pain and guilt I had been carrying in my life since forever. For Mr Tony was right that it was not the woods that were the real problem but the pain and the guilt that was deep enrooted within us? The guilt of not saving my loved ones that grew with time and made our lives a living hell. The woods were just helping us to see the truth and the truth was embedded inside us. The fear of losing happiness made the woods appear dark and wild. FOR, THE WOODS WERE NEVER DARK BUT IT WAS US WHO WERE DARK INSIDE.

The stars were twinkling in the sky and were somehow barely invisible through the branches above. I was now not scared of anything, not even of being caught. It felt as if something was so light in me. I was still sitting at one spot while Mr Tony was gathering some twigs and branches to light up a fire for the night since it was getting cold with time and we were not going to leave by tomorrow. He collected some dry grass to make a bed for us two to sleep on as bedding. Also fire was important to keep the wild animals away from us if they were any. I too started collecting fire fuel by now to help him a bit. He then lit up the fire and we warmed up ourselves. We were hungry by now having nothing to eat so we tried searching for something edible around us. Mr Tony found a few berries that he said were usually common in the woods so we had them though they weren't sufficient to ease our hunger but it was enough to at least help us not go empty stomach to sleep. So we both slept closer to each other so that we don't die of cold while fire burning next to us surrounded by stone to avoid being spread around.

It was midnight now. The fire was off by now but there was coal still burning and ignited by the breeze moving all around. I felt a bit cold and I woke up to light up the fire again. So I put on some firewood to ignite it and then I was just going back to sleep when I saw someone standing on the opposite side of the fire from a distance. It was a boy faintly visible in the dark, unable to be recognised but he seemed like someone I was in search of for so many days. It was my Tim, standing there still looking at me and then someone came from back in white gown, the ghost of the little girl, she took his hand and he started following her as they vanished into darkness.

"NO, JUST STOP TIM! PLEASE DON'T GO WITH HER!" as I shouted to stop them.

I was just getting up to follow them when the old man woke up from his sleep by my voice and held my arm to stop me on time. I looked at him only to ask him to leave my arm but he didn't.

"That's not him. Please accept the reality. You need to be strong," as he looked into my eyes trying to ease me.

I hugged him tightly and cried my heart out. It was the last time I saw him and I couldn't even stop him.

I felt so shattered and completely devastated and the pain was penetrating deep inside me and tearing me apart with all the memories coming to my head. The old man consoled my broken heart. And then we tried to sleep again, although I couldn't really sleep thereafter. The noise of the crickets whispering in the woods was disturbing the silence. And my constant thoughts and memories were adding on to the perplexity of the scenario.

I remembered how Tim used to get scared by my stories and still used to hear them up just to keep me happy with my creations. If he would have been with me now he would have been sitting up all night just to keep the coal burning so that I don't catch a cold like the other day when I wasn't keeping well, he still woke up from his deep sleep just to fetch me water. He was a loving kid and he deserved the world and all the happiness. But I failed to offer him what he deserved. And now here I am sitting alone at this place just to keep him in my memories. I wish he gets a good life in the next birth which he always aspires for. But what was I going to say to his aunt who still was dependent on the poor child's earnings? Or did it really matter to her even? If he was alive or not if there was no money involved? Maybe, no, she never loved him or did she care about him. But what did I do to him? I also didn't keep him safe and now I sacrificed his life just to keep up with the insecurities of my life. For I was the real devil now as the world was calling me right at my face what I really deserved.

I looked at the tall trees above my head. They seemed to be vanishing into the sky, they were no longer scaring me with the darkness. I could see the woods turning brighter as the night was bid bye by the morning light. It was like a fresh morning and I could hear some early birds chirping in the woods. The truth was revealed, the secret was unfolded by now and the woods were appearing so normal to me at the moment as if nothing had ever happened before. Mr Tony was awake and I had brought a fresh hunted squirrel for breakfast since there was not much to eat other than berries around. Though I had never really hunted in life before, this morning seems to have served me well for no reason. We lit up the fire to roast the little meat and then we finished eating it to add some food into our almost empty bellies. We then planned to warm up a bit and then in a while, move towards the outskirts to leave the town and meet Joseph, who was supposed to be waiting for us on the other end of the woods with his vehicle along to help us flee from here. Mr Tony had already told him about all that had happened and he was ready to help us and get us out of the town as soon as possible. We now started moving towards the other end to get out. But before moving Mr Tony and I had a pledge in there; a pledge, to let go off things and to forgive all to release them of any pain or guilt. The most important promise we made that day was to ourselves that we won't hold on to the past and also we must free ourselves from the burden we had been carrying since ages filled with guilt and remorse. I knew this day was new and fresh, a fresh day to start our new lives. I knew this was the last time I would ever see my brother. But this was how things were meant to be. Maybe he would have wanted the same. He would have wanted me to live a happy peaceful life with no regrets. So I walked off from the land of sorrow to start new beginnings for my brother to smile up there in heaven.

I love you brother for being the best companion of my life. And the little things you did to make my life a heaven on Earth. You made me enjoy every moment of my life. You made me live my life better. I could still sense you around me. I felt like turning back for once and so I looked back to bid him the final goodbye. He was there, he was there smiling through the woods right back at me and this time I smiled back to let him know he meant the world to me. Sometimes it's not easy to let go of things that hurt you but when you let them, you accomplish the most soothing feeling of lightness that you feel inside your body. The feeling of ease, the feeling of new you, that makes you alive.

I left my sorrow and pain behind in that town that helped me know the real me. So now I don't hold any grudges against them and I want God to bless them indeed. Mr Tony was walking in front of me and he seemed the most sorted person I had ever met. My perspective was changed and I was viewing the world through a new lens. We were about to make through all our sufferings and our happy lives were waiting outside the jungle, outside the town. That's how happy endings are.

But wait, what about the town people? I almost forgot to tell you about them. The story is not yet finished so hold on a little more. Not all stories have happy endings. Let's see what happens next.

The Final Summit

We kept moving, thinking about our journey till date and smiling through all odds to start fresh and new. I was sure that I was going to meet Mr Tony in future too for he was the only good thing, not a thing but a person I earned through all this mess - a good friend and a great supporter. Though I found a new me too, that was the most important thing till now. But wait things were changed with us but not the people of the Viva City.

Yes they were all hunting for us since yesterday and now the only place they would last search for was the woods. So they were behind us looking desperately for us to quench their thirst for revenge. We were unaware of their presence in the woods already. So we were moving at a normal pace. Mr Tony had once again contacted his brother in law, Joseph to inform him about the time we would take to reach him. And then we heard something and that made us immediately hide ourselves behind one of the trees having large trunks. Someone was there and I couldn't afford to get caught at this stage when we were so near to escape out of this hell.

"They must be hiding in here somewhere. KEEP LOOKING," commanded a heavy voice that seemed to be of the sheriff.

Our expression of relief had now turned into a serious one. I looked towards Mr Tony for our next move and so did he. He then signalled me to run away without being noticed before they reached us. I thought we were supposed to run together but as I turned back I saw him still hiding in there. So I stopped, it was us making it happen all together till now so I couldn't leave him behind at this crucial point. So I went back to pull him towards me but he instead pushed me away and asked me to leave. I too became reluctant to go and this could turn into a failure of our plan. I was struggling to pull him along and Mr Tony was having something else running in his head. He said that he had a plan and I had to trust him anyhow so I decided to go on my own.

I could hear someone following me so I just decided to turn to see who it was but suddenly something hit my head hard and I fell down on the ground with my eyes faintly looking at the man who had hit it from the back. I couldn't understand why he did so and then my eyes completely closed. I could hear noises around. People were yelling and screaming all around and it all appeared like a dreamy feeling. I didn't know what happened next exactly. My brain took me long back to the guilt that I had been holding all the time. It took me ages back to the time when I too had a happy family to live with and enjoy with.

****

I could see her floating in the air laughing her heart out. My Susie was right in front of my eyes as I recalled how energetic she was. Then I saw her dancing in the rain. Her innocent little smile made my eyes teary and my heart melt. But then I saw something I never wanted her to do. I saw her losing her calm at petty things. I saw her taking things and words to her heart and mind. She was becoming a rebel day by day. She had so many questions unanswered in her head that were turning her furious over petty things. You know how kids are stubborn at times, so was she. She had now started messing up with our father often with things that ultimately were resulting in her getting punished. Mother often tried to resolve her queries but they were never ending but growing more in number with time. Susie wanted to be considered like her elder brother. She wanted to enjoy the bicycle and not Barbie games. She loved hanging out with other kids in the neighbourhood playing games like cricket, football and so on. But father wanted her to behave more like a girl. He often used to scold her for asking things I had to play. He would say that she was not made for those things. This disheartened the young mind.

It was one night when the argument between the two worsened and my father took her to a dark store with no light in it. He locked her up there for around fifteen twenty minutes to give her a lesson for life. I stood outside the door just watching things happen. I thought Susie might cry or ask for help but there was utter silence from inside. Father just opened the door to let the kid out since he felt he was harsh on her. And yes it did work as a lesson for her but only in a worse manner. She now knew that they had no answers to her queries and she wasn't at fault for being such a curious child. But she started hating her father after this incident and now this caught the attention of my sweet mother. My mother loved her the most but now she had to take the case in her hands for her own sake. So she decided to not be lenient with her. Whenever Susie came up with her curious questions or rebelled, her mother would not let her sleep with her. Susie was a young kid afraid of sleeping alone in the dark. She would never let the lights go off to help her with her fear. I never thought about how these things were heading to her mind. She started losing interest in being with people now. Also she no longer wanted to play with my toys or do my stuff. But her questions were still there.

Like always she came up with one more rebelling opinion on the dining table. This made the father furious and he left half eaten from the table. I saw him frustrated but not reacting in anger and then I was quiet minding my own eating business. I then saw my mother clench the dining table cloth with anger for the first time. She lost her calm for the first time. I never saw her furious before and then she yelled at the kid.

"Don't you get it? Enough … your behaviour is not going to be tolerated here. Take your food and go to your room. Eat there alone and sleep there alone!"

And then she looked at me with a red face filled with rage.

"Don't you help her now onwards? Let her be on her own. She thinks she knows everything and she wants to know everything. Better not help her in any way."

She left the table and I saw Susie sitting opposite to me, her eyes filled with tears. I finished my food and left. She was sitting there all alone. She went to her room. Sitting and sobbing over being left alone with her lights on. It was a stormy night that day. It started lightening and thundering and that was making me worry about her. But I wasn't supposed to help her out. I was lying down in my bed and my eyes became heavy so I slept. Susie was sitting on her bed thinking about all that everyone had done to her. It was midnight now and mother had cleaned the utensils and kitchen and they were off to sleep with a heavy heart. But all she was doing was to make her a better person. She turned on slow music to have her daily routine of lullaby for them. My parents always went off to sleep with slow music on. So they all slept that night except for the little girl. She was still up and suddenly the thundering sound made her freak out for a moment. Her eyes were still in tears. And then there was a power cut. Nobody noticed since everyone was asleep by now. Susie couldn't bear the pitch dark room and she fled from the room straight away to her parents' room. It was dark in the corridors and the window was open with rain water coming inside. She slipped down and fell hard on her face on the cactus plant to which she screamed. Her voice was almost suppressed by the thundering outside and the music played in the room of two. My room was quite far from the two so I barely heard the scream since it was raining heavily outside. She got up with those thorns pricking her face, still sticking to her. Alas! Her face was bleeding badly; they were so deeply embedded. She had hurt her knees so bad that she tried crawling on the floor with baby steps to reach out to her mother's room. She thudded their door for help, crying in pain.

"Mommy, please open the door. I fell in the dark, it's hurting."

The mother woke up and she was about to get up to check on her daughter but the father held her arm. She looked back at the father to which he nodded his head and asked her to sleep.

"Better not open. This is how she will learn."

My mother was quiet for a moment. Her eyes were filled with tears but she tried not to be soft this time so she slipped back into her bed. She could hear her daughter crying and banging the door to open but all she could do was to control her emotions.

And then my mother said something which she could never forgive herself for-

"If you won't behave next time, the henchman will take you away with him and teach you a lesson in his own way."

The henchman was an old guy living in the neighbourhood being deaf and dumb. All kids could never relate to his sign language and used to be scared of his very sight.

She was still banging the door. And then suddenly it stopped. There was no beating of the door heard anymore. Mother got worried a bit and for a few minutes she waited but then her anxious motherly love took over and she got up to see if everything was alright. She tried turning on the lights but the power cut was there and this made her worry more with guilt added to it. She opened the door, but there was no one standing outside. She took a torch out of her side table to check in Susie's room as well as she might have gone back after so many failed attempts. She went to her room and there was nobody there which led to her anxiety. She was frozen in fear and started calling out for Susie but there was no response. I heard her voice coming near my room which woke me up. I went outside to check what was happening. My mother and I searched for her everywhere but she wasn't there. Even the main door was locked from inside so there was no chance of her going out in the dark. She fled towards her room to inform my father. I followed her hurried footsteps since it was dark and she was bearing the light. And then we reached her room. But suddenly she stopped at the doorstep and didn't move.

"What happened mom? Let's just inform father. What are you thinking? Hurry, just open the door."

But she didn't move even an inch, so I crossed her to open it myself.

And then a scream was heard so loud that day that the whole town must have heard. I cried that moment with tears rolling down my cheeks and my face turned red in pain and despair. My father opened the door to see his wife standing pale with tears rolling down her face and his son crying abruptly out so loud and then he saw mother looking at the door handle outside the room to which were clinging the fingers of the little girl holding on tight to the handle. It was just the fingers left behind. That day I saw my father cry so real bad that I stopped for a moment. It was still raining outside. I could hear the sirens of the police vehicle outside our house. They searched the whole night for the body but couldn't find one. It took days and months for them to close the case as there was no evidence found, no clue what had happened with her. My mother never spoke to us thereafter. For her, it was her fault for leaving her baby in the dark. My father was devastated by this incident and he gave up his job. I knew how painful it was for them to even hold guilt for letting her suffer. They never forgave themselves for all that happened. My mother ended up in depression and one day when I came back home from work, I saw her hanging to the ceiling fan in my room. I tried saving her, my father did. But we couldn't save her. I cried my heart out that day. I screamed out so loud. I burst into tears, my world ended so soon.

SHE WAS GONE! SHE WANTED HER DAUGHTER SO BADLY THAT SHE WENT BEHIND HER IN HEAVEN! AND NOW SHE WAS GONE…!!!

Years later my father died of a heart attack although by now I had learnt how to live with pain. I held myself together to be a person my father always wanted me to be. I followed his footsteps and became a bestseller author tying up with magnificent publication houses. My name rose with time and work. And here I was working on my dreams. It was a few years later that I found an angel again in my life, my Tim, who was now everything for me. He was my family, my world and my hope to smile each day looking at him living his life. And I couldn't bear to lose him now at any cost. I never want him to leave me alone here in this dark world filled with despair and pain. I fell in love with him at the very first sight and things fell in place for us to live happily till now. And now what!!! I lost him!!! Did I? Maybe I lost myself SOMEWHERE... FOREVER! GOODBYE!!!

****

"Sir, wake up, are you alright?" I could hear a voice faintly trying to bring me back to my senses. An old man unknown to me was visible through my faded sight. I could see the clear sky above my head and there happened to be no trees covering it. I had never seen the man before and as I struggled to get up with his help I could feel the pain on my head where I was hit. But the man introduced himself to be Joseph whom we were supposed to meet at the end of our run. I was still half conscious and tried to look back from where I came. All I could see was the woods on fire erupting flames and fumes. How did I get here? How did the woods catch fire? And what happened to Mr Tony then? My eyes were stuck in the woods still trying to regain my consciousness and trying to recall what exactly happened. But it was of no use. I couldn't remember a single thing after I got hurt.

"Just don't stress yourself much. Come with me let's go now," as Joseph helped me while walking towards his car.

"But, where is Mr Tony? What happened to him?" asked the anxious me looking at the woods while moving slowly.

"He was a great man, if it wasn't him you might have got caught by now," said the old man.

"But I saw him hit me with that rock in his hand. Why did he even do that to me?" while I gave him a perplexed look.

"He hit you because he saw that the sheriff had already seen you. And he was ready to shoot you down. So he pretended that he was on their side so that you wouldn't get killed. I had almost reached there but hid myself behind the tree since Tony wasn't taking my calls and that made me worried. I saw what all happened there. The sheriff thought that you were dead and so did the other clan. They were about to take you to their town but that wasn't what Tony wanted to do and in order to stop them he lit up a matchstick and saw that the whole ground was full of dried twigs . He dropped it while nobody noticed his move. And then the whole place caught fire and they left the body there to save themselves. It was then I came to rescue you from behind and took you out of the woods with the help of Tony. But the sheriff hadn't left yet. He saw Tony helping you out so he called him a traitor and tried to kill him with his gun. But till then they ended up fighting with each other and a gunshot was heard behind us. Sheriff had shot my friend Tony by now and it was us next on his hit list. But Tony was still having some life in his body and the courage in his heart so he just strangled the sheriff and he fell off with his gun dropped next to Tony. So he took the chance and he eliminated the leader to break down the clan. Though we lost him there, he wanted you to be safe. So, here we are next to each other," Joseph in a low tone.

I was numb by this time, things were moving so fast and blurry in front of my eyes as Joseph continued narrating the whole scenario. Why did he have to die to let me live? The woods were gone now and so were the beliefs. There was no returning back but we lost so much in there to just discover the new beginnings. Maybe that was the necessary part and so was the story of the brave kind hearted old man who gave up his future to enlighten others' world. It's him who made the story end in a better way for people around. I went with Joseph to the city to his place and stayed there till I was okay to return to the real world. While the town back also had some misconceptions broken with all that happened and with time they learnt to create happiness within rather than searching in other things or people around. For the forest, new saplings grew up in place of old ones marking the beginning of a new era and new world.

FOR NOW THINGS ENDED WELL LIKE ANY OTHER STORY AND THAT'S HOW I GOT

THE PLOT OF MY BEST SELLER. But this time it wasn't for the sake of earning materialistic wealth and appreciation but it was for all those loved ones we lost in the process. It was for all the new lives that were born that day. It was for all the young hearts and minds that revived and learnt to live a happy contented life on their own. It was for my family, for my parents, for Susie and last but the most important one my love, Tim.

TO LIVE WITH PAST IS TO LET YOUR PRESENT DROWN AND NEVER SEE FUTURE AGAIN. So this journey made me build a world full of acceptance and growth. The day we accept things, the day life becomes easier and happier too.

Epilogue

5 YEARS LATER, I managed to start up my own publication firm. Things were pretty well with a new connection of mine, Joseph who too had an interest in writing business and new ventures. We were partners now, helping up new writers to bloom with their creations.

"Didn't know I would come this far from all that happened years back!" exclaimed me in general talk with Joseph sitting next to me.

We were both in a new place, in a new town – Dreamland, a place for several wannabes residing in there trying to make the best of their lives. Joseph was still an oldie and Goldie with no companion for life. I wonder how he managed to live on his own with no family around all these years. But to me he was like someone I would have definitely cherished. He was someone who too had lost so far but gained a lot in the process. For us destiny played a crucial yet traumatising role but now we were happy to start a new journey with no regrets added to our memories anymore. We had each other's back and that is how things were turning great for each one of us.

"Don't you feel like settling down," Joseph asked me in a teasing tone.

"I am already settled up and just following your footsteps," as I giggled back trying to play along with him.

"Oh come on, start up a family soon so that I can at least see your children as my grandchildren you know. Come on enough of your work and business now," laughed the holy old man in a notorious manner.

"And that's the reason you are single till now almost turning your seventies I believe," as I tried to give him back but in a joking way.

We both had a hearty laugh since we both were having similar notions regarding getting married in life. I was happy to have him as my family and so was he. Joseph was a great man and I couldn't deny following his footsteps. We have just shifted here a few months back and it was giving us immense help to grow our market here where there had been only us as a publishing house. Things are great for us at the moment with happiness making its way into each one of our lives. Also my previous series success had made me quite popular worldwide with fans walking up to me every single day from all over the country and sometimes globe too.

Joseph loved seeing the fans more than I did. For him it was like a new thing to brag about in the town. We were making a lot of money out of our business and we loved what we did.

Like any other day, we were having our afternoon tea when we both heard the doorbell chime.

"Well let me see, maybe one of your fans again," Joseph got up excited to address the uninvited visitor.

I was still sipping my tea while recalling the time when those little hands served me the best tea in the world. I smiled, as I could still see him smiling back at me through the air. Joseph was at the door and then he opened only to find nobody standing outside.

"Who's that?" I asked him with a loud voice from a distance.

Joseph was looking around but then turned back to nod that there was no one there.

"Maybe someone is playing along. Today's kids you know, how they are," Joseph was about to close the door when he noticed a box lying outside on the floor. He took it inside with him and was opening it while walking towards me. The box had no name on it. He then sat down next to me to see what was in the box, and he got an envelope in it.

"How crazy people are with no sender's address or anything neither on the box nor even on this envelope," Joseph sighed in complete disappointment.

I turned towards him to see what he was talking about. All I saw was a white envelope he was holding in his hand and was just about to open. When suddenly something struck my mind and I stopped him and asked him to handover the envelope. I am not sure what made me do that but it was some kind of impulsive move that I had no idea about. I opened the envelope and found a letter which read-

DEAR FRIEND,

I AM GLAD YOU CAME. LET ME WELCOME YOU TO OUR WORLD. I KNOW YOU DON'T KNOW ME BUT LIFE IS TOO SHORT TO HAVE REAL INTRODUCTIONS MY FRIEND.I COULD HAVE WISHED FOR A BETTER FUTURE FOR YOU BUT YOU ARE ALREADY BEST AT YOUR PRESENT. MY WRITER FRIEND, STOP GUESSING NAMES WHO IS WRITING TO YOU. THAT'S NOT SO IMPORTANT TO KNOW RIGHT NOW. BUT I AM HERE TO HELP YOU LIVE BETTER AND LONGER THAN YOUR STORIES THAT YOU SELL OFF SO WELL. THERE IS A SECRET I KEEP... A SECRET THAT I WANT YOU TO KNOW SINCE YOU ARE ALREADY HERE. A SECRET THAT WAS LONG BEEN KEPT AND CONTINUES TO STAY WITH ME.

THERE IS SOMEONE OUT THERE.SOMEONE SO UNREAL YET VERY POWERFUL. SOMEONE LOVES TO HUNT. SOMEONE LOVES TO TEAR MINDS APART. SOMEONE IS THERE LOOKING FOR YOU. THERE IS SOMEONE WHO WON'T SPARE YOU AT ANY COST. SECRETS ARE DEADLY, DARK AND DEEP. DON'T PEEP INSIDE. REMEMBER, DON'T LOOK BACK. JUST SAVE YOURSELF!!! I SAID... JUST SAVE YOURSELF!!!!!

YOUR WELL WISHER

(THE SECRET KEEPER)

What did I just read? Was it real? My face had turned pale as I just ended the letter. I read it twice to ensure I read it correctly in the first place. A strange familiar feeling started taking roots inside me again after so long. Who could have been behind this now? What else did I have to lose now?

"What's written in that?" I heard Joseph enquire.

I looked at him in shock and a perplexed state with cold sweat running down my back.

"NOTHING"...........

———————————————————————****————————————————————————